SPACE FLEET SAGAS

A Collection of Adventures

BACK STORIES PRIOR TO THE
LAUNCH OF THE SFPT-109, JOHN F. KENNEDY

DON FOXE

CABALLUS
PRESS™

ISBN: 978-0-9988044-2-2
ISBN: 978-0-9988044-3-9 (e)

Library of Congress Control Number: 2017906873

Acknowledgments

When I first began writing down the stories for the novels it became clear some important details would be glossed over. To fill in the blanks, I offered a short story, novelette, or character sketch on my website, donfoxe.net, each month.

Those rough back stories designed to help a reader better understand how Earth, Space Fleet, and the galaxy reached the point of SFPT-109's launch in Book One, *Contact And Conflict.*

This collection takes those early short works, cleans them up considerably, and places them in chronological order.

As promised to faithful followers, I have also included a never-before released novelette, *Convergence.*

Author's back cover photograph courtesy of *Abri Kruger Photography*, South Africa.

Special thanks to LtCol Art Parker, Ret. Marine Aviator, UH-1N "Huey" -- for taking time to provide insight and suggestions regarding Rapid Response Mission Planning and military aviation tactics.

A pat to Silus, my Greater Swiss Mountain Dog who passed away suddenly, only three months after faithful Zeke. The house seems huge without them.

THE ADVENTURES

CONCEPTION
Setting: Mars.

PANDEMIC
Setting: United States of America

NIGHT EAGLE
Setting: Sardinia / Algeria

THE RAID AT AJEJ
Setting: Tunisia

THE SPACE RANGER PROJECT
Setting: Nevada, US Western Can-American Union

CONVERGENCE
Setting: Tampa, Florida / Iran

Contents

CONCEPTION

(Original Title: Discovery and Destiny)

*My fascination with Mars is a reflection of our collective
desire that Mars holds the key to our past and our future.*
DF

CONCEPTION appeared in OMNI magazine, APRIL:
2017.

"The first real step in the colonization of Mars occurred when the Fairchild Corporation developed their version of a sealed bio-dome construct," Winnie said. The
Brown University doctoral-grad student sat in a comfortable
chair facing the window. The Martian landscape of Gale
Crater stretched to a hazy red horizon. The blue sky of early
morning fading into the soft butterscotch color that dominated the spectrum during the daylight hours.

"Fairchild's bio-scientists introduced colonies of oxygen-
producing cyanobacteria and algae. The combination created
an oxygen-rich atmosphere with a high probability of repro-
duction from Martian soil."

She spoke to fellow archeology student, and Martian
rookie, Maury Ackerman. More aptly phrased, she talked
aloud in Maury's presence.

The tall, gangly Ackerman kept his eyes on the red-
desert, rocks, and changing sky laid out before him. Whenever he looked directly at Winnie, her large breasts clearly
outlined in a tight t-shirt caused him to lose focus. Or, more
to the point, over-focus. They partnered on research projects
at Brown, but Maury rarely ventured into the field. If he had

known Winnie wore a lot less clothing away from campus, he might have gone to sites more often.

"The system could harvest oxygen to support humans living in controlled habitats, and save billions of dollars in costs associated with Mars missions," she continued.

More than a pretty co-ed, Winnie Henderson vied against top candidates from archeology departments around the world to join Mars Mission Number 6. Her Ph.D. would be waiting for her return.

Maury just as smart, proven by being the other student selected, but less driven. His family's money, and D.C. connections, contributed to his inclusion on the mission.

They shared an interest in extraterrestrial archeology. They did not share an interest in each other.

"The second breakthrough occurred when scientists at Fairchild Industries' research and development subsidiary in Saudi Arabia, used the same cyanobacteria to produce food and fuel sources. If you did not have to ship food or fuel from Earth to Mars, billions more in cost savings made developing a habitat worthwhile."

Maury knew the history of Mars habitat. Everyone knew. He let Winnie continue. She was actually working through portions of her thesis. She often tested thoughts out loud. He did not mind, as long as he could see her with his peripheral vision.

"The final breakthrough, the one to deliver a sustainable Martian colony, came when Basin Aerospace in Nevada designed a retro rocket capable of controlling the landing of large ships in the shallow Martian atmosphere. A rocket-system weighing significantly less than past types."

Winnie leaned forward, looking at Mars, imagining Earth and the recent past. Maury looked at her, hoping to glimpse side-boob around the sleeveless t-shirt.

"The Fairchild Corporation, with additional funding by several governments, as well as private agencies, began the construction of large cargo boxes at the orbital space station. Well, actually, first they needed to expand the space station to house construction crews and equipment."

"The Ackerman Group provided some of the funding," he said. He wanted to remind her he came from money, and his family's history with the project. Looks were never going to get him close to her, but looks did not count for everything.

"They needed to build cargo boxes, which could double as space ships, and become pre-fabricated homes once they landed on Mars. The applied engineering required to design and construct these multi-functional units would compete with the advanced principles used to build the pyramids as humanities' greatest example of innovative thinking."

Winnie sat back again. She marshaled her thoughts, putting cold facts into more interesting terms so her thesis might also, one day, become a book.

"The boxes required rockets capable of getting them and their payloads to Mars. Installation of the new Basin retro rockets guaranteed the cargo ships could land safely. Technicians had to imagine, design, and build computers able to operate throughout the trip, and subsequent missions. Robotics, which could set the stations and systems in place, needed to be repurposed from other tasks."

Becoming a little tired of Winnie's monologue, Maury decided he could show a bit of his own Martian historical knowledge.

"Fairchild Industries constructed twelve cargo ships. They would launch from the Earth Moon Space Station. Seems like someone could have come up with a better name," he added.

"I suppose EMS2 is a little better than ISS, for the previous International Space Station. They could have called it Skywalker Platform. Or the Enterprise Station. Maybe something spooky dark, like the Void Terminal."

He turned to see if Winnie appreciated his humor. Her scowl indicated she did not.

"Those cargo ships, designed to morph into habitats, were built over a ten-year period," he said, trying to remove the scowl by returning to the original discussion.

"During that time, advances in propulsion resulted in rocket systems converted from liquid-chemical to ionic sublight engines. The new power plants proved faster and safer than chemical-fueled rockets. Metallurgists invented lighter materials, incorporating properties to shield humans and equipment from radiation. Radiation is much more dangerous in space, and on Mars, than on Earth."

He mentally kicked himself. Every school kid knew radiation was more dangerous in space.

A male voice joined the discourse.

"Ten years of planning, construction, and after more planning, the ships were sent on their way. A 250-day journey, thanks to the new ion-engines. The twelve ships landed on the surface. They touched down one by one, via computers operated by techs at the Fairchild Control Center near Indianapolis. The landing site selected because it was an open valley where solar panels could get plenty of sunlight. The other factor for setting up shop in the Gale Crater was the sixty-percent chance of ground water hidden below the dusty, red surface."

Elliott Fairchild stood behind the two. His attention on the view, but his thoughts ranged millions of miles and past years away.

The two college students remained in awe of Fairchild. Hero-worship not diminished by the time spent together on the planet. They listened reverently, as he continued the tale.

"The ships were interconnected, forming a large square. Next, pre-fabricated light-weight carbon-steel beams were released. They extended to form the ribs of an umbrella over the square's open center. Translucent radiation-repellant cloth got rolled out, and robotic arms stretched it across the metal skeleton, enclosing the center."

He moved his eyes to Winnie. "It's your paper. What happened next?"

"Robots set up the cyanobacteria system. Heaters began to warm the Martian soil beneath the cargo ships and new bio-dome. Algae introduced to help fertilize, and rejuvenate the covered soil. Unmanned rovers deposited twenty solar-panel units outside of the prefabricated habitat, and ran fiberoptic cables back to junction boxes on the exterior of the cargo ships. This provided the energy to maintain viable conditions within the habitat."

Winnie ended her point-by-point descriptions. The history of Mars Habitat engrained in her memory, and available on demand.

Not to be over-shadowed, Maury took over. Unable to make eye contact with Fairchild, and fearful of stumbling if he looked at Winnie, he faced the landscape.

"After six months, readings indicated Mars had a village suitable for sustaining human life. Plants were even taking root in the reclaimed Martian soil. Pumps brought water from an underground river, 200-yards beneath the surface. Filtration systems made it usable."

"It was time to launch the Fairchild Aerospace Martian Expedition. FAME 1," the thirty-year-old aerospace engineer, planetologist, and grandson of the man who started

Fairchild Industries said with a catch in his voice. That first launch, with people on board, and their incredible mission, so enthralled him as a child, it shaped his future.

"Dr. Fairchild, you are one of the engineers who helped design the current ships used to transport people and supplies between Earth and Mars," Winnie said. "What was the first ship like? Ares One."

He smiled, recalling the model of Ares One displayed on his bedroom dresser as a child. It now sat on a credenza in his office on Earth.

"The Fairchild/Basin Spaceship, Ares, was a large, winged vehicle designed for flight within an atmosphere, or in the harsh conditions of space. She used jet propulsion for lower-atmosphere flight, and ion sub-light engines for space travel. The ship could sustain a dozen people for a year, and had a load capacity of 60,000 pounds.

"The mission crew?" she asked.

"The twelve-person crew consisted of pilot, co-pilot, scientists, engineers, and one physician. They signed on for a three-year term. Six months of space flight to Mars, and another six months to get home. A two-year stay on the planet.

"Once the astronauts arrived, and set up shop on Mars, they became huge celebrities on Earth. People from around the planet watched twenty-four-seven live steaming video on pay-for channels. Universities and science labs paid for special access to information and data. They were given the opportunity to ask the engineers and scientists on Mars to conduct experiments for them. News agencies paid for interviews, and magazines ran biographies and family photos.

"One internet Billionaire offered the very beautiful, and very stacked biologist, Dr. Maila Elg of Finland, one-million dollars if she would publicly shower on his pay-for porn site. She refused. Until the offer reached five-million, and a percentage of revenues. Over one-billion people worldwide tuned in for the thirty-minute shower scene. Dr. Elg was set for life when she returned to Earth."

Fairchild turned from the view to look directly at the two archeologists.

"I was one of the children on Earth caught up in Martian fever. Old novels, and movies about Mars and Martians became the rage," he confessed.

"Can I ask one more question?" Winnie asked, now turned in her seat to better see the mission commander. On his nod, she said, "I know you initiated the program to select two archeology students for this mission. I also remember from the interview, you believe life once existed on Mars. Do you expect us to find anything that would indicate a civilization did exist?"

"We know life existed on Mars," he replied. "Whether a sentient civilization ever developed is purely me speculating. Even if it did, after millions of years, I doubt there is anything left. But human's always hold out hope, Winnie. You and Maury are modern-trained archeologist. On Earth you use the latest technology to help make a best guess at where a lost civilization might have built infrastructure. Utilizing current topography, with computer-generated maps of how landscapes once looked, you determine geographic hot spots. I expect you to do the same on Mars. Imagine what a living planet looked like a million years in the past. Assuming civilized Martians existed, where would they build?"

The antique chronograph on Fairchild's wrist gave a barely audible beep. "If I hadn't fell in love with space, I would have studied archeology," he told them, and left.

Maury watched Winnie watch Fairchild walk away. He wondered if her hero-worship ran deeper than fan-girl fascination. "His name has taken him a long way," he said.

Winnie presented him with another scowl. "He received degrees from universities renown for the specialties he pursued, including two doctorates, one in advanced engineering from M. I. T. , and one in planetology from Stanford.

"No one complained when Elliott Fairchild was selected to head the sixth Mars Mission. With his credentials, no one considered nepotism played any part in his position as mission commander.

"That man is more than qualified to lead any extra-planetary exploration. His expertise regarding Mars, as well as the advanced life-sustaining systems built for, and developed at this base are well documented by science-based publications around the world."

The co-ed gathered her belongings, gave her fellow Brown student the cold shoulder, and departed, hips in full sway.

Maury watched any hope of hooking up while on Mars march off with her.

———————

Ares 3, a ship capable of housing thirty people for two years of space travel, launched from the Earth Moon Space Station on July 1. FAME SIX off to a good start, with a Mars arrival ETA planned for January 1st.

The ship landed two days earlier than expected. It departed ten days later, with fourteen returnees, and storage spaces filled with mineral samples, plants, and experiments for study or completion on Earth.

Elliott Fairchild watched it go with no regrets. As far as he was concerned, he was home.

The day after Christmas, Boxing Day, one Earth-calendar year later, Fairchild stepped into his cabin from the attached head. His long brown hair still damp, having just towel dried it. The towel now wrapped around his narrow waist. At thirty-one, he was of average age on Mars, where the majority of the people living on the planet feel into the late-twenties to early thirties category. Considered studious and academic since early childhood, he also enjoyed sports and exercise. His body remained as toned as his mind was sharp.

"You look yummy," remarked Kati Ikonen, doctor of botany, and twenty-four year old daughter of Dr. Maila Elg, famous for her Martian shower scene. Kati displayed all of her mother's curves, and inherited her flare for science, though she preferred botany over biology.

She also picked up her mother's adventurous nature, so signing up for a three-year stint on Mars had been a no-brainer. Convincing the handsome young Fairchild he should spend time with her in bed offered no obstacle.

"Don't you ever get enough?" Fairchild asked, teasing the woman still buried under covers.

"Nope," she answered. "It's the lower gravity and the higher oxygen content," she explained. "It makes me bouncy-bouncy."

"Well, while you bouncy-bouncy in the shower, I need to get dressed, and get going," he said. He leaned over to kiss the blonde, blue-eyed vixen. "Dr. Castro simply cannot wait to get to that mountain he keeps going on about."

"Geologists," Kati said, throwing off the covers to reveal a body made for holo-magazine covers. "They all have rocks in their heads."

"Old joke," Fairchild replied.

The mountain, now called Mount Sharp, originally designated Aeolis Mons. The prominence located west of the center of the Gale crater. The Mars Habitat in a direct line east, across the crater, near sites visited by the first Martian robotic rovers in the twentieth and twenty-first centuries.

The mountain rose 18,000ft, so not nearly the tallest on Mars. It had been the subject of a couple of studies over the decades. Many Mars' mountains were volcanic in nature, and some extremely tall. The magma run-off piling up over centuries, then cooling over even more centuries. Mount Sharp was different. Believed to have been created by sedimentary erosion over a half-billion years. The top of the mountain rose only 3,000-feet above the crater rim. The official planetologist with the team thought the crater once contained a giant lake. With the basin filled, The top of Sharp would have become an island, similar to those found in giant lakes on Earth. Whether Sharp's creation occurred before the lake, or after it disappeared remained undetermined.

Mount Sharp had a consistent slope of three-percent. During the warmer months, salty water ran down the slopes to the base.

What excited Dr. Benjamin Castro, mission geologist, about Sharp involved a relatively flat surface exposed by a huge wind and subsequent sand storm that blew through the crater earlier in the year.

"The wind blew away a million years of debris. It removed a lot of the residual brine that settled around the western base of the mountain," Castro said to Fairchild. They rode together in an enclosed multi-wheel transporter.

"From 1,000-feet up there is now a ninety-degree drop, instead of a three-percent slope. It's also over 2,000 feet wide at the base. It's as if someone took a trowel and scraped a sand dune's side flat."

"You think this proves Sharp wasn't created by sedimentary erosion?" Fairchild asked.

"I've only had a short amount of time on site, but the face of the rock, all the way up to the 1,000-foot mark, appears to be uniform. If erosion alone created the mound, there would be strata indicating when erosion, or buildup occurred."

"So what are you getting at?" the team leader asked.

"Straight surfaces rarely occur in nature," Castro replied. "This might be an indication sentient life once existed on Mars. Someone could have carved this section, creating a flat space. Who knows, it might once have held murals, or might have been the back wall for a structure."

"For hundreds of years people on Earth have dreamed of Martian neighbors," Fairchild said, trying not to jostle too much as the transporter rode over rough terrain. "I believe Mars was once a living planet. We have proof of water, rivers, lakes, oceans, bacterial life, and even some plant fossils. But if it supported a civilization, it happened millions of years ago. The thought we would discover anything created by an intelligent being so long ago still existing today is fantasy. It just isn't going to happen."

"All I need is a chisel mark. Anything indicating a tool did this," Castro replied. "It's worth taking the time to look."

"I agree," Fairchild said. "Otherwise you would be alone with the driver, the mechanic, and the two archaeology students."

"We're on the mountain now," the driver informed them. "It'll be another half-hour to get around to the wester slope."

The placement of the morning sun sent shadows running before the transporter. The vehicle did not encounter many large boulders. It did, however, need to travel through an abundance of debris. Plenty of small rocks and pieces of pulverized planet drifted down the slope, or were blown across the base of the mountain. It made for a bumpy ride, but the transporter was built to cross every type of obstacle Mars threw at it.

Comfort, however, had not been an engineering consideration. Designed to traverse the landscape, and protect occupants by shielding them from radiation. The transport contained provisions for a week away from the main habitat.

The driver, a retired sergeant in the British Royal Marines named Toole, handled the big vehicle with ease. He enjoyed access to all of the driving luxuries, such as power steering and automatic transmission. The cabin provided air-con and heat.

The sortie's mechanic, Lee Hampton, rode the shotgun seat. A black man from Tennessee who learned his trade at the factory constructing Mars transporters and several other military-grade vehicles. No expedition left the bio-dome without a mechanic. The SOP saved more than a few trips from disastrous endings.

Fairchild and Castro occupied the bench seat behind the driver. Behind them sat the two archeology students from Brown University in Providence, Rhode Island. The two doctoral grad-students earned a research grant, and seats on FAME SIX, for a joint paper submitted regarding potential digs on Mars. Their suppositions based on satellite scans of the surface, combined with penetrating radar images providing anomalies to ten-feet below the surface. The Gale crater, and Mount Sharp ranked high on their list of potential sites.

Winnie Henderson tried to downplay her appearance by not wearing makeup while on location. She kept her brown hair cut short, and dressed for functionality.

She lost the battle to remain understated because her breast filled her t-shirt. Since she refused to wear a bra, they bounced when she walked and performed a tango when the transporter lurched.

Maury Ackerman was tall (six-three), and gangly (one-forty-five), with greasy black hair pulled into a ponytail. He tried not to stare at his companion's chest. He lost this battle quite often.

"You can start getting into EVA suits," Fairchild said over the back of his seat to the students. He gave a sneaky look at Winnie's round rear end when she moved around the bench seat to the rear of the transporter.

The double-high rear section of the transporter allowed a person to stand up, and get into, or out of light-weight EVA coveralls. The baggy suits worn over civilian clothes.

After tugging on her suit, Winnie changed places with Maury, who was careful not to rub too hard against her as they crossed paths.

By the time Castro and Fairchild changed, the transporter reached the dark side of the mountain. Toole parked in shadows, precisely at the coordinates provided by Castro.

He and Hampton would remain in the vehicle unless needed.

The four in back slipped on helmets and gloves. They checked rebreathers, and inspected each other's outfits to make sure all seals were closed. Toole pressed a button, and a plastic shield slid down to separate the driver's compartment from the rest of the transporter. The expedition team could now exit or reenter the transporter, getting any materials needed, without having to constantly vent the atmosphere.

Castro and the archeology duo headed straight for the wall. Fairchild took a more leisurely stroll around the base.

While the trio used lamps, magnifying glasses, soft-bristle brushes, and laser scans to inspect the face of the mountain, Elliott would use the time away from the habitat for private reflection. He enjoyed his journeys away from the biosphere. He enjoyed the time alone. Mars, away from the habitat, provided the perfect location for someone of solitary nature.

The team stopped for lunch back in the transporter. They returned to their exploration as the sun swept over the top of the mount, lighting the western slope. Fairchild, a half-mile away, walking the crater, and inspecting it for signs of water erosion, turned and faced the mountain. From here, with the sun shining brightly, he could see exactly why Castro had been excited. A portion of the mountain looked like a screen from an old-fashion drive-in movie park. Maybe there stood the answer. Gale crater had been a parking lot for an alien drive-in movie theater.

He returned to the slope. He could see Castro at the mount's far right base. The geologist waddled on his knees, shoveling away debris. The lanky Ackerman walked across the base with a tape-measure in hand. Henderson, who even filled out her EVA well, and had Fairchild thinking long, and hard about Kati waiting back at the habitat, held the other end of the tape.

"It does look like a flat screen," he said, once he reached Castro.

"Elliott, look here," Castro implored him. "Look," he repeated.

Fairchild squatted to see what Castro fussed over. The geologist cleared an area of debris and sand, revealing a square, twelve-inches by twelve-inches, outlined against the rock wall. A hand print appeared embedded in the center of the square. The design clearly displayed four fingers, and a thumb. The design obvious; neither worn down, nor a trick of shadows.

"Oh, my, god," Fairchild said. "Benjamin, you just uncovered the single most important thing ever found on Mars."

He pounded the Chilean geologist on the back. He activated his com mike, and requested everybody else, including the driver and mechanic, join them.

"It looks like a palm reader. The kind once used for security doors," Hampton said. "A few doors in the older sections of the space station still use something similar," he added.

"Should someone place a hand on it?" Winnie asked.

"No," Fairchild warned. "The atmosphere will bleach your skin raw. Right now we take as many photos as we can. You two (nodding at the students) can use your infra-red scanners to see if there is anything interesting nearby. We will need to mount another expedition. When we return we will   bring whatever scanners, radar, and sonar we have available to discover what might be over, under, or inside of this mountain."

While Fairchild made plans, Castro knelt before the square. He placed his gloved right hand into the imprint.

"It can't be human," he said aloud. "Yet, my hand fits inside the outline."

The rumble warned them first. Then the entire planet seemed to shake. A line formed along the base of the mountain. Loosened rocks and shale started falling form the sky.

"Jump," Fairchild yelled. At twenty-eight percent of the gravity of earth, the six of them leaped a good thirty-feet away from the face of the mountain. "Keep going," he said. "There's 17,000 feet of mountain above us, and it could all start coming down."

With leaps and bounds, they escaped toward the sun, traveling a mile before stopping, turning, and looking back.

The massive transporter disappeared into a cloud of red dust.

The giant flatscreen had recessed into the mountain. They watched the entire wall slowly rise like a garage door.

"That ground shake had to be monitored at the habitat," Fairchild said. "The door going up is shaking the whole mountain. If we don't get back to the transporter to call in, they'll be sending ground and air support soon."

That was the practical thing to say. The impractical thing to say would have been something like: *"Holy, crap! A giant door has just gone up on a Martian mountain, and there may be something inside not been seen in over a million years!"*

Exactly what Fairchild was thinking, if not shouting.

"What do you suppose is in there?" Winnie asked. "Do you think anyone has survived?"

"If you ever told me you believed in a Martian colony hidden beneath the surface of the planet, I would have had you kicked out of school," Maury said. "Right now I wouldn't be surprised if a little green man stepped out and told us they didn't allow solicitors in the neighborhood."

"That pad wasn't for security," Hampton said. "Damn thing was a doorknob."

"Look, it's stopped," Castro pointed out. "And the mountain didn't come down. Do we go in?"

"What if we go in, and the door comes back down?" Winnie asked. "There might not be a doorknob inside, and nothing says the one on the outside will work again."

"Dr. Castro and I will go in," Fairchild said. "But we only go in a few feet. Toole, you, and Hampton make sure the transporter is functional. Winnie, you and Maury will stand at the entrance, and keep your torches on us. If the door starts down, everybody get the hell away. In fact, if the transporter is okay, move it out here. Get it into the open. And let base know we're okay. Do not let them send out another team. Not yet."

The six started back, with Toole and Hampton veering off for the vehicle.

At the entrance, Winnie and Maury brought out high-beam torches, and shown them into the cavern.

Nothing but darkness and deeper darkness appeared in the artificial glare. Fairchild and Castro added their lights, and still nothing became obvious.

Castro yelled "HELLO." It echoed for a long while. "Big," he said. "Quiet," he added.

"Maury, hand me the measuring tape," Fairchild ordered. "We only walk in until this runs out. Then we come back." He handed the mechanical end to Maury, taking the tip in his gloved fist. "Let's go, Benjamin. This is your cave."

Fifty-yards inside they no longer needed their flashlights. The cavern slowly began to brighten. The light permeated the entire inside of the mountain. It emanated from the interior walls. Recognizing their presence, illumination not used for eons came on.

Fairchild and Castro stood absolutely still. In front of them, pointing at the entrance, rested a flying saucer. The ship appeared to be a football field wide, and one hundred-feet tall. It sat serenely, nestled in a space rising for thousands of feet, and back, beyond the rear of the saucer, for thousands more.

"It isn't a cave," Castro said.

"It's a hangar," Fairchild replied.

END

PANDEMIC

Our planet has been united before. Alexander III did it, if you do not count the western hemisphere. Rome kind of did it. No one expects a single leader to ever unite the planet. For over two hundred nations to accept a central governing body, something dramatic, probably tragic would need to occur.

DF

(Timeline: Nine to Thirteen Years following the discovery of the hangar and space ship on Mars.)

Oval Office

"Can you back up a second?"

President Arthur A. Tamiroff, seated in his wingback chair, scrolled across the information airdropped to his secure data pad. The daily security briefings, normally frightening, just elevated into spine-chilling.

"What were those two departments, and what the hell are they?" he asked his Director of National Intelligence (DNI).

An aide to the DNI normally presented the President's Daily Brief. Director Constance Patterson presented the PDB today. Tamiroff's Chief of Staff, Henry Long, the only other person allowed in the room.

"Global Emerging Infections Surveillance, the G E I S at the Armed Forces Health Surveillance Branch, A F H S B is a section of the Department of Defense, D O D."

"I fucking know DOD, Connie," Tamiroff barked.

Patterson ignored his growl. She and the Armenian-American attended Boston University together. They both completed law school and worked their way up the government ladder. He went into elected politics, and she became an intelligence superstar. Twenty-four years after meeting in Intro to Poli-Sci, they sat in the White House, two of the most powerful people on the planet. Tamiroff's bark never compared to Patterson's bite.

"I wasn't being snide, Mr. President," she assured him. "When I start calling out acronyms, they become infectious."

"Infectious," Long repeated. "Seems to be the word of the day."

"GEIS operates an integrated worldwide emerging infectious disease surveillance system. They monitor a global network of reporting stations specifically trained to watch for any regional outbreaks with potential for worldwide implications. They also support research initiatives for drugs, or other innovations to protect our people. Specifically, to protect US military personnel and dependents stationed overseas, but their work eventually keeps everyone safer."

"Where's the CDC on this?" Long asked.

"They concentrate on public health inside the borders," Patterson replied. "They have international connections, but nothing as sophisticated as GEIS."

"And they believe the current outbreak in China isn't natural?" Tamiroff asked.

"They are the best in the business, especially with respiratory diseases," the DNI replied. "Most people don't know they exist, but they have been the first to detect, predict, and develop strategies to prevent the spread of global respiratory diseases since the MERS and SARS outbreaks in the late twentieth century. The outbreak in China is a weaponized version of Clostridium difficile, or C. diff."

"Give me the short version, please," the President said.

"The average human digestive tract is home to as many as 1,000 species of microorganisms. Most are harmless under normal circumstances. When something upsets the balance of these organisms in your gut, harmless bacteria can grow out of control, and make you sick. C. diff is the worst of the worse. Toxins released in the intestine by C. diff cause severe diarrhea and abdominal pain. There is a loss of appetite, fever, and internal bleeding if not treated quickly."

"Sounds like an abdominal disease, not a respiratory disease," Long remarked.

"GEIS determined C. diff in China is being spread through air-born contact. It also does not respond to antibiotics."

"Why would the Chinese weaponize, and release a lethal disease inside their own country?" Tamiroff asked.

"Population control," Long answered before the DNI could. The Chief making the logical jump before the President. "China has a population of over two billion, and growing. The government has been fighting social and economic problems associated with overpopulation for decades. And losing. Overly populated regions have led to the degradation of land, diminished resources, pollution, and horrid living conditions. Riots occur daily. Death by starvation is hidden, but rampant."

"The Chinese government introduced a weaponized version of C. diff as a desperate attempt at population reduction," Patterson concurred, and concluded her brief.

"What can we do?" the top executive asked.

Long answered. "Nothing. Short of releasing the GEIS conclusions, the problem is a Chinese problem. If we claim the government is actively killing its citizens, it won't end in a war of words. It will cause a real war. The Chinese government is not going to admit to mass executions. We're talking about the people who have annexed everything from the Sea of Japan to the Bay of Bengal over the past one-hundred years."

"They've relied on nation-building to increase access to the natural resources and agricultural land needed to support their population. It's caught up to them. They cannot support the people they've conquered, and their own people." Patterson continued. "The world stood by when they built islands in the South China Sea, and claimed territorial waters. That first step lead to a progressive takeover of country after country."

Long interjected, "Now bordered by Russia, India, Japan, and Europe, China cannot grow without starting a global war."

"But killing their own people?"

"The old, the weak, the poor," Long said. "Correct me if I guess wrong, Connie, but a disease that causes severe diarrhea will have deadlier results among those with weaker constitutions."

"Correct," Patterson replied.

"If it is weaponized, the people at the top will have a cure in hand," Long surmised. "No way they would release an airborn plague where they live, unless they were immune."

"Logical," Patterson agreed.

"So we do nothing," Tamiroff said. "We let them kill off a few million of their weak, sick, old, and poor, and we do nothing. How in hell can I ignore the truth?"

"We don't ignore it," Long replied. "We let them know we know. We'll let them cull some of their population, hell, they've already killed a few million. We tell them to provide the cure. They can act like they have come to the rescue of their ailing citizens. And we get concessions."

"Use the fact we know they are murdering their own citizens as leverage in future negotiations?" POTUS looked at his Chief of Staff, wondering if he knew the man he had known for two decades.

"You don't have to like it, Mr. President. But it's the way international politics have operated since tribes decided to fortify borders. Right, Connie?"

"Doesn't make it right," the DNI replied.

Oval Office

"Do we believe them?" Tamiroff asked.

Four weeks later, another PDB followed up on the GEIS analysis of the C diff. outbreak engineered by the Chinese government. Again presented by his Director of National Intelligence, with his Chief of Staff present. The private briefing delivered more dire information.

"They gave us their data. That's how frightened they are," Patterson told him. The DNI normally appeared cool, calm, and in control. At 7:45am EST, she appeared to have been awake all night preparing the daily brief. A single-subject brief. Considering she had not slept more than four hours in the previous forty-eight, she looked pretty good.

"Armed Forces Health, the CDC, two private agencies under threat of the national security secrecy acts, and our biological warfare experts have all reached the same conclusion. The weaponized virus the Chinese developed to spread C diff. mutated. The cure they developed for the original strain does not work. No antibiotics work against a virus. No current treatments will be effective against the mutant C diff. infection."

"What about natural immunity?" the President asked.

"Some, but only a few cases reported," Patterson replied. "They bio-engineered the disease, and designed it for airborne transmission. The mutated version is more virulent than the original. People are wracked with agonizing abdominal pains, fever, and uncontrollable diarrhea. Seventy-five percent die within forty-eight hours. Right now, half of those not killed directly by the infection, die of related causes."

"Eighty-seven percent death rate? Seriously?" POTUS asked.

"Higher among the young, old, and anyone already sick. The only good news is about twenty-five percent of the Asian population targeted appear to have natural immunity. We're sending teams in to see if they can find out why. Information they recover could help find a solution," Patterson continued.

"You're being awfully quiet, Henry," Tamiroff commented.

"Tell him the rest," Long said to Patterson.

"It's spreading. Global transportation means global pandemic. The analysts predict two-thirds of the world's entire population will be wiped out. Three-hundred million American citizens will die unless we act immediately."

"Act how? You said there isn't a cure."

"Close the borders," Long answered. "We need to contact Canada and Mexico, and get them on board. If we act immediately, with force, and without giving in to compassion, we may be able to stop anyone else with the virus from entering North America. Once we close the borders, we contain outbreaks inside the country."

Tamiroff turned back to his DNI.

"Connie, straight and simple, please."

"Mobilize all armed forces, including National Guard. Restrict entry to a couple of airports and sea ports. People and animals on board international flights, or ships at sea remain quarantined seventy-two hours before allowed entry. Anyone attempting to enter the United States otherwise is aggressively stopped."

"Aggressively meaning?"

"We shoot down planes, sink ships, and kill anyone trying to cross on foot," Long answered.

"If Canada and Mexico disagree?" Tamiroff asked.

Patterson answered.

"We use the old Trump wall with upgraded security sensors. Activate autonomous weapons along the Mexican border. We station armed soldiers, utilize satellites, and deploy drones along the northern border. Armed ships in the Great Lakes, and armed boats on the Rio." Patterson looked at the Commander-and-Chief with tired eyes. "They'll agree with us, Arthur. When they see what will happen if they don't, they'll agree."

"The coastlines will be impossible to cover," the President argued.

"We recall every naval ship and submarine. We need to get those people back and away from potential infection anyway. We blockade the Atlantic, Gulf, and Pacific coasts from on, over, and under the surface. Behind them, we station Army, Air Force, Marines, and National Guard."

"Alaska, Hawaii, and the protectorates?"

"Tell them to use whatever equipment we can leave behind to do the same, but pretty much on their own," Long replied. "Islands will be more secure. Alaska could be a nightmare. I can see Asians attempting to escape by crossing into Alaska."

"We have military installations, embassies, and Americans in every corner of the planet," Tamiroff argued. "What about them?"

"Order all military installations into lock-down. They can institute similar quarantines before allowing American citizens entry. If an outbreak occurs inside an installation, we can't help them," Patterson answered.

"The State Department can order everyone to the nearest military base, but I would require the quarantines now. It's already too late to take risks. We will arrange airdrops to keep the installations supplied. They must to be prepared to use lethal force to repel locals. When the pandemic hits, people will panic and try to find the safest place."

"If we start shooting planes down, the American people will revolt," the President argued. "The press will report every action. Splash photographs of innocent victims. I'll be run out of office."

Henry Long brought the meeting to its conclusion. "Mr. President, you have to declare martial law, activate all military forces, and close the borders. You have to do it now. If you wait, there won't be an America. The Joint Chiefs are aware of the Eastern Pandemic. The options given to you by Connie are the responses agreed upon by every military, intelligence, and medical analyst we have. History will record you had no other option. The future is about to change, but if we do not go to war against this attack, there will be no future for anyone. Make the call, Mr. President."

PEOC

The President's Emergency Operations Center (PEOC) is a bunker-like structure. Located beneath the East Wing of the White House, the PEOC serves as a secure shelter, and the communications center for the President of the United States.

One year after the initial briefing on the potential for a worldwide pandemic, the Eastern Pandemic's spread resulted in three billion dead. One-third of the world's population fell to contagion.

"The number is an estimate," Patterson said. "Over half of the planet's governments are non-functioning, or partially functioning under martial law. No one is worried about counting and announcing the number of dead."

"The other half?" Tamiroff asked.

"Trying to survive," she replied. "The smaller island nations are having a better go at it. The United Kingdom and Ireland have the military resources, and the will, to keep their shores closed. Japan, with the help of our Seventh Fleet, closed Honshu. There are hundreds of smaller Japanese islands, real and artificial. Each one is responsible for itself. Australia and New Zealand were both in trouble the last time we heard from either. Too close to Asia, and too easily accessible."

"Europe?"

"Scandinavian region operating, and almost everything south getting hit hard."

"Middle East?"

"Israel shut the borders at the first hint of the pandemic. The IDF (Israeli Defense Forces) are aggressively maintaining separation. The majority of middle eastern or northern Africa nations are not broadcasting any news. Back-channel reports from those regions are discouraging," The DNI said.

"The Sixth Fleet moved command from Naples to Sardinia. They've transferred all fleet assets, and secured the island."

"Did Italy object to Vice Admiral Murphy stealing their island?" Henry Long asked. Long lost over twenty pounds in the preceding year. He wore borrowed military fatigues, and looked scruffy. The Chief of Staff looked out of place in the underground version of the Oval Office. President Tamiroff wore a suit and tie. Connie Patterson dressed in a crisp blouse, and A-line skirt.

"The Vice Admiral explained to the Prime Minister, if they wanted any assistance from the United States military, they needed to use their military securing the mainland, not attempting to retake an island the Fleet needed to borrow."

"Africa?" The President continued his list, not actually hearing the replies. They were going through the motions, and all three knew it.

"Devastated. There's a large Asian population of merchants, mining operators, and consultants throughout the continent. They flew in family and friends in an attempt to keep them from getting sick. They brought the sickness with them. A lot of small pockets of armed groups, often tribal, or ex-military units, have established no-contact zones. They don't come out, and they do not let anyone in."

"Asia?"

"Two-thirds of the population dead or dying," Patterson replied. "Our biggest potential threat is angry militant assets with access to advanced weapons, planes, ships, and even orbital satellites. It's every nation, province, city, village, and person for themselves. Anarchy. Chaos. US military forces in Hawaii, Alaska, and the West coast confront refugees representing every Eastern culture several times every day."

"And?"

"The quarantine stations became death houses," Patterson reminded them. "People rioted, broke out, infected entire sections along the Pacific Coast."

"I remember," POTUS said. "I don't need a reminder. The US military forcing American citizens to remain in those infected zones. Opening fire on people who disobeyed."

"It was necessary," Long chimed in. "Everything we have done has been necessary to save the country."

"We haven't done anything, Henry." America's first Armenia-heritage president buried his head in his hands, rubbing his fingers through thinning white hair. "We stay safe in this underground city beneath Washington, and we issue orders. Correction, I issue orders. Those orders result in people dying."

"Did you hear Connie?" Henry demanded. "Two-thirds of the Asian Pacific population are gone. Their unburied bodies creating even more bio-toxins, threatening to kill those left. Gangs with modern weapons, and no controls, taking anything, anyone, they want. The United States and Canada have lost less than twenty-five percent of our people. Most of those on the coasts, and mostly because kind-hearted people could not turn sick refugees away. Your orders have been the one thing keeping this country viable."

"The country is surviving," Tamiroff acquiesced. "But we have lost our soul."

"The soul only matters when you're dead, Arthur." Long crossed his feet at the ankles, and studied his dress shoes. Perhaps noticing how odd they looked with army fatigue pants, and olive drab socks. "We're trying to keep people alive. If the country survives, they'll be time later to find religion."

POTUS turned back to Patterson. "South and Central America? Mexico?"

"Refugees turned away by our military went south. Some nations set up strong coastal boundaries, and some did not. Bottom line, sporadic enforcement and containment from the US-Mexican border to Patagonia.

"Mexico was in good shape, part of the Canadian-US-Mexican combined defensive posture, until dumb-ass criminals started taking money to smuggle people in-country, and bastard politician, cops, and military personnel took bribes to look the other way.

"We had coyotes attempting to bring them across, into Texas, Nevada, hell, all along the southern border." Connie set her data pad down. She knew the stats without it. POTUS did not care about them anyway. "When Border Patrol and the National Guard realized, they closed it down, hard. They assigned armed guards along the old Trump wall, released drones, armed heli-hovers, and turned on the Autonomous Weapons System. The AWS fires lasers on anything within ten feet of the border."

"Patrol agents and Guardsmen went beyond the wall every day for over a month to burn the bodies," the Commander-and-Chief recalled. "The press went crazy. Smoke from mass pyres streamed live."

"We should have muted the press long before then," Long said. "Trying to allow freedom of the press during martial law was our worst decision. Nothing we did ever good enough. We weren't finding a cure quick enough. Martial law was illegal. People were suffering, and they needed to show it in brilliant definition."

"The research?"

Patterson shook her head at the President's inquiry. "Every military, government, public and private lab with the facilities to discover a cure are working on little else. That's true here, in Canada, and every nation we still have contact with. The Irish have some of the best pharmaceutical labs in the world, and finding a solution is priority one. Over one hundred incredible medical breakthroughs have occurred as a result of the research, but no cures, and no immunizations."

"How long can we survive?" Finally, the big question.

"Incredible as it may sound, the vast majority of our people are supporting your efforts, Mr. President. The nation is energy independent. We can produce enough food to take care of ourselves. The government is a pared down version of itself, but we are operational. The military is backing us, and that makes all the difference. State and local authorities are following your lead.

"Canada is experiencing the same thing. They have a much smaller, more homogeneous population, and a much smaller military, but their nation is holding together. Having a unified ally to our north, and a strong border to our south makes it easier to maintain security."

"Can the military hold out?"

"I say yes," the nation's top intelligence agent replied. "We have some smart people at the top. The units stationed on the coasts confront, and eliminate threats constantly. The generals, and admirals for all branches have worked out rotational schedules to assure no single unit is forced to deal with those decisions for too many days without a break. We relocated military families to safer installations, mostly in the mid-west. That helped ease tension among the enlisted. They have a job, and a goal. It keeps them grounded."

"Mars?"

"The people on Mars are self-sufficient. They have the spaceship and hangar to keep them busy, and we are still able to send supplies occasionally. They may be the safest group in the solar system."

Nevada Proving Grounds / Secret Military Base

"They believe they have a vaccine?" President Arthur Tamiroff, seated on an office chair, in his work space, four levels beneath the Nevada desert, scrolled across his data pad. He scanned the recently tap-loaded information delivered by his National Security Director, Constance Patterson.

Twenty-eight months after Patterson's first PDB hinting at the potential for a pandemic, twelve months after POTUS departed Washington, DC for the security of the Nevada installation. With an estimated four-point-five billion dead, he did not want hope dangled falsely.

"The lab in Indianapolis has been running tests for over a month. Last week Seal Team operators infiltrated known infection areas. They inoculated survivors without symptoms, and people dying from the Eastern Pandemic infection." Patterson never looked at her own pad. She spoke directly from memory. When she received the news, it seared its way into her being.

"We have an immunization against the disease, and a cure. When the cure is delivered within twenty-four hours of the initial infection it is one-hundred percent effective."

"It will work?" POTUS would ask until he believed.

"Yes. We would have developed a cure years ago if the Chinese had been honest," she said. "When they first came to us for help, after the virus they developed for population control mutated, and their cure became obsolete, they swore they gave us everything on how the weaponized C. diff had been created. Everything except their splicing the Marburg virus into the C.Diff matrix."

"Marburg?"

"Marburg virus, or MARV causes Marburg virus disease in humans and nonhuman primates. It's a deadly, eighty-percent fatal form of viral hemorrhagic fever. It's a rare disease, usually associated with bats. When people contract MARV, it's transmitted by contact with another person."

"Scientists did not see this sooner?"

"C. diff also causes fever. Everyone associated the hemorrhagic fever in Eastern Pandemic cases as a result of the weaponized C. diff mutating. A primate disease specialist in Indiana noticed something familiar on a research slide. When he passed along his report, it led to the discovery the Chinese bio-tech designers piggybacked MARV and C. diff. It opened a new path for research."

"Now what?"

"Now we convert every pharmaceutical plant into a manufacturing facility for the vaccine. We save the world."

"Connie, we can put this out to the public, yes?"

"Yes, Mr. President. I'm sorry Henry did not live to see it happen," Patterson added.

"Stress," Tamiroff whispered. "It's killed a lot of our colleagues. It's killing me, as well."

"You can let it all go soon, Mr. President. The way you kept the nation functioning, the people alive, and the government operating will be the topic of poli-sci lectures for centuries."

Tamiroff allowed himself a small smile. It was foreign. His facial muscles unfamiliar with the movement. "You've been my rock, Connie. From the beginning, your counsel, and your support have help steady my shaking hands. But I honestly cannot continue. My doctors tell me I have to call it quits. My body is breaking down."

"Who would you appoint as a replacement?" she asked. "The VP died from the Pandemic years ago. The Congress disbanded by the Martial Law directive. Now is not the time to put a general, or admiral as the leader of the nation. People will need to see civilian control return."

"That is why my final official act will be to sign the Can-Am merger. We've discussed it for more than a year. It makes sense, the two strongest nations left on the planet, both historic democracies, having joined forces to present the Eastern Pandemic from destroying our countries, should merge. It will be the first step in an effort to unite the remaining populations under one governing body."

"I know of the discussions, and I agree with the logic, but is now the time. Now when we have a cure to deliver?"

"Best time ever, Connie. The Prime Minister of Canada is younger, healthier, and a good woman. She will be able to use the vaccine as a gift, a prize, or a threat to make the nations which still have leaders join the discussion for uniting the planet."

"You think big, Mr. President."

"Do you know the Hindu deity called Shiva?" he asked.

"God of destruction," she replied.

"What most Westerners think," Tamiroff said. "He is also the Hindu god of creation. They believe for creation to occur, something else must be destroyed first. In every destructive occurrence, a seed of creation is present."

"The Eastern Pandemic destroyed the world we knew." Connie Patterson grabbed and held her friend and President's line of reasoning.

Tamiroff completed the logical, spiritual, and eventual conclusion. "To replace what was destroyed, we must create a United Earth."

END

NIGHT EAGLE

(This short story occurs concurrent and following the events in *PANDEMIC*.)

Facts:

- The US Navy's Sixth Fleet is stationed in Naples, Italy.
- Sardinia is an Italian-owned island east of Naples.
- Constantine, Algeria, known as the City of Bridges, is one of the most beautiful sites in North Africa.
- All characters and events are fictitious. Any similarities to real people or events are coincidental.

A story is only captivating if the characters are believable, sympathetic, despicable, or just plain interesting. They can have super powers, come from other worlds, or be the girl next door, but they have to touch you, the reader, or the story falters. I have written background-history pieces on nearly every character in all of my books. Slowly I am turning those pieces into stories. This is my personal favorite.

DF

SARDINIA

"Toni, you have to stay here. If your father calls or gets through, you need to be here for him and your brother."

The cargo hover-copter awoke with a hum from the power plant. The sound low, warm, and reassuring. Michele Paré, wearing a grey flight suit with no insignias, not even her Captain's bars, sat behind the left yoke. Her eighteen-year-old daughter stood beside and behind her, between the pilot and co-pilot seats.

"Mom, you can't go alone. You can't leave me here alone," she said.

She pleaded once more to accompany her mother. An appeal repeated regularly since learning of the desperate plan to locate Toni's father and younger brother.

The two remained somewhere on the Italian mainland. Vice Admiral Murphy's emergency order to redeploy the entire Sixth Fleet to Sardinia included setting the exact time for the last ship to sail. Anthony and Michael never made it to the fleet-assigned docks in Naples. When the last ship sailed, anyone not aboard would need to find another way to escape the Italian mainland.

"Your father and Michael will be at the farmhouse north of Naples," Michele told her daughter. "That was the plan. If we ever got separated, we would head for the Ricci's farm. I can fly there, get them, and return in a couple of hours."

"And get courtmartialed for stealing a Navy hovercopter," the younger Paré added.

The Naval ships, over-filled with personnel, support staff, and families, disembarked the District of Capodichino base on orders issued out of fear. Fear the spreading pandemic, having arrived on the European continent, would be too difficult to defend against with the city of Naples surrounding fleet activity headquarters.

Vice Admiral Murphy, without express consent from the Navy, ordered the emergency relocation to southern Sardinia. The twenty-four hours required for the relocation created chaos, but no panic. Military people and dependents drilled for emergency removals. Forced evacuation was a potential fact of life for anyone stationed overseas.

"Maybe," Captain Paré said. "But if it means Anthony, Michael, and you are safe, I'll happily pay the price. Now get off the copter. Stay by the sat-link com unit. I'll stay in touch.

You need to listen for your father. If he contacts you, let me know where they are."

The tall, slender teenager gave her mother a quick kiss on the cheek, backed out of the cockpit, and jumped down from the side door to the tarmac. She ran a couple of steps and turned. Brilliant green eyes, damp with tears, watched the shuttle lift on compressed air. Her mom smiled and waved.

She returned the wave, continuing the gesture as the hover-copter flew across the asphalt and concrete, the shoreline, and out to disappear over the blue Tyrrhenian Sea.

SARDINIA
(Two Years Later)

"Paré! Just what-the-fuck do you think you're doing?"

Naval Flight Officer (NFO) Turner Irving stood with hands on hips, feet spread, and face twisted into a countenance guaranteed to bend wills, if not steel.

"I am not a fucking aircrew trainer. I train pilots, Paré. You ain't a pilot."

"I'm not aircrew either, Ty," the twenty-year-old countered. "I guess I'm just a mutt."

When her mother never returned, and her father and brother never made contact, Antoniette Rachelle Paré became a ward of the US Navy's Sixth Fleet. It was not an official designation. She simply became one of hundreds of armed services dependents caught alone in the aftermath of the deadly contagion coursing across the planet.

Vice Admiral Murphy basically invaded Sardinia, and annexed the port of Cagliari on the southern tip of the island. Marines maintained control of a large triangle encompassing the docks through the south-central section of the town.

Armed Marines allowed no one into the restricted area without extreme caution.

First, they had to be US citizens, and, second, they would spend a required two weeks, minimum, in a special quarantine facility.

When the virus jumped from the mainland to the island, restricting access became deadly. Panicked islanders trying to escape the disease forced military personnel to fire. In the beginning they fired water hoses or rubber bullets. This escalated to gas. Finally, deadly force. People also tried sneaking in from the water and by air. Every attempt turned back, sunk, or shot down.

During the two years following her mother's unauthorized departure, Toni Paré underwent a transformation. The giddy, light-hearted teenage girl became a stern, no-nonsense young woman.

She dealt with loss by filling her time working for the Navy. No job needing done seemed unimportant. If the cooks needed a dishwasher, her hands drowned pots and pans until her skin burned red. If garbage needed incineration, she was there. She acted as a clerk in administration, and cleaned weapons for the armory.

She also learned. She learned close quarter combat from the Marines. She practiced with every personal weapon stored on the base. She was good at both.

Very good.

The Warrant Officer in command of small arms training called her 'the most natural shooter' he had ever seen. She simply did not miss.

No one needed to teach her how to fly. Her mother, a decorated Naval pilot who flew everything from hover-ships to the latest super-sonic exotropospheric fighters, taught her daughter to fly before she could ride a hover-bike. She continued to hone those skills with a flight simulation program stored on her computer. The 3-D sims helped her escape the pain that threatened to tear her down any time she allowed herself a quiet moment. It kept her close to her mother's spirit.

The NFO's face untwisted. This young woman had become family. Her insistence on helping around flight operations, and her ability to fix anything capable of flight made her an indispensable member of his staff. The loss of so many people, from the virus, to the hurried relocation, and the desertions following setting up shop on Sardinia, left every section short-handed. Paré filled a lot of needs for a lot of commanders, but no one received more of her time than NFO Irving.

"Toni, you can't go 'round calling yourself a mutt," he said. "It ain't fair to dogs."

"Rachelle," she said.

"What?"

"I prefer people call me Rachelle." Toni was the name of the girl who lost her family. Toni laughed, danced, and wanted to become a teacher. Toni hurt all the time. Rachelle was none of that.

"Okay, *Rachelle*. Changing your name don't suddenly make you a pilot," the NFO said.

"Lt. Simmons is the pilot," Paré said. "You're sending her on a support mission to Malta. Malta is one of the few places on Earth completely free of disease. It is also under attack by renegade Italian sailors trying to fight their way ashore. Every possible copilot is already out there, or too exhausted to stay awake. Ty, you know I can handle the second seat. Simmons can't fly, shoot, and watch her own six, even with the advanced computer systems. I'm here. I'm qualified. You decide."

Irving boasted thirty-plus years in the Navy. The thin, ramrod straight black man from Kansas intimidated everyone who came into his sphere of influence, including those of higher rank. Except one skinny, brown-haired determined twenty-year-old.

"Go, but Toni . . . sorry, *Rachelle* . . . if you get killed out there, don't you dare come back here."

Rachelle Paré strapped into the right seat of the fighter. Lt. Simmons, herself only a couple of years older, welcomed the help. It was not the first time Paré sat next to the pilot.

She begged ride-alongs whenever she could. She knew the routines, and she knew the systems.

DAHLONEGA, GEORGIA

At the same time Rachelle strapped into her seat for the flight to Malta, on a secure US Army Ranger training facility near Dahlonega, Georgia, USA, an eighteen-year-old Daniel Marcel Cooper stood before his father, Colonel Peter Cooper.

"You sure?" the elder Cooper asked.

"I am. I want to enlist," Daniel replied. "Going to college now makes no sense. With the new Can-Am-Mexico alliance, the military is going to be important if the world is going to survive. When they find a cure, someone will have to deliver it. After the pandemic is stopped, the whole world will become a war zone. I'll do a lot more good as a soldier than a student."

"Can-Am Alliance," the elder Cooper corrected. "Mexico can't control the cartels trying to slip refugees into North America. They've been cut out of the alliance. Your Mother would have wanted you in school," the career Army man added.

"She would want me to make a difference."

"You can enlist here, but I have no idea where the army will send you for training."

"Doesn't matter. As long as they train me, and put me where I can help."

CONSTANTINE, ALGERIA

(Two Years Later)

"Thirty of our guys northwest of the airport, backed against a ravine," Ivanov told Coop.

Serg monitored coms while Coop used the night vision on his scope to track the action around the Boudiaf Sky and Space Port.

The two formed a crew-served sniper team. Specialist (SPC) Daniel Cooper did the shooting, and PFC Serg Ivanov acted as spotter, support, and protection.

Their current assignment to a Can-Am Force Recon company of one hundred-twenty Rangers started the same way their previous dozen missions began. Hurry up. Wait. Drop into unknown territory and fast-foot to a hot zone. Wait. Shoot or don't shoot, and get out.

Then all hell broke loose.

"That would be the western fire teams," Coop replied. "Eastern units have assembled with the northern teams." He set the rifle down. The weapon wrapped in gunny sack cloth to keep it safe from the dirt and sand. "I can't see the South from here. Anything on sat-rad?"

"Just the guys northwest, and their radio signals are sporadic," Serg responded.

The Russian sat with his back against an artificial dirt-bank created decades before when the Algerians built the N79 highway. He faced abandoned buildings. The airport-spaceport facility lay east of their position, on the other side of the roadway.

Coop lay atop the rise. The position provided line-of-sight over the entire airport, as well as most of the flat farmland around the tarmac.

Sat-rad, short for satellite-fed radio system, allowed the units and individuals on the ground to remain in touch at all times. It also allowed the company to stay in communication with home base in Tunis, Tunisia.

"Makes no sense," Coop said. "We should be able to talk with and hear everyone."

"Jammers," Serg answered. "Not the latest or the best, but good enough to cause the sporadic results."

The Can-Am Rangers were on site at the request of the Algerians. Constantine, a beautiful city, and once the home to 750,000 people, needed help. Former army soldiers from France arrived after the cure for the pandemic had been distributed. They laid siege to the city's 125,000 survivors. Using military hardware and tactics, the French mercenaries killed the few remaining police and militia. They set up command and control at the former air and space port, and began demanding taxes from the population. Intimidation, rape, and murder followed.

The City of Bridges became a city of fear. The reforming government in Algiers agreed to join the United Earth movement, if Can-Am agreed to remove the French infidels choking Constantine. They estimated between two-hundred and three-hundred heavily armed former armée de terre. These military-trained opportunists used the port facilities and adjacent hotels for headquarters and garrisons. From these fortified locations, they ventured in and around the city framed by ravines. Constantine was accessible primarily by bridges.

The bridges, for vehicle and train traffic, and the river remained guarded twenty-four-seven by members of the self-titled Brigade Nouveau. Armed patrols kept residents in, visitors out, and maintained a close watch on all activity around Constantine. With mobile antiaircraft guns stationed at the spaceport, the New Brigade maintained control of their fiefdom.

"Algerian Intel reports two or three-hundred former French army grunts," Coop said. "We get dropped five miles east, trek across a desert valley, in summer heat, divide into four fire and depression units, and surround the port. We're outnumbered, but we're trained, and coming in before dawn to surprise them. Sneak in, hit 'em before they know they have company. Clean up the outliers next."

"They actually number closer to two-thousand than two-hundred, and our guys walk into a beehive," Ivanov finished. "Hold on, Coop. Getting something through from another unit." The former Russian commando closed his eyes, which did not help him hear better. He cupped his hands over his ears, which did.

"The combined northern and eastern groups are under the A1-N79 junction. Using the concrete for cover." Ivanov opened his eyes. "Forty total. That means twenty KIA or MIA. They are surrounded. Incoming fire heaviest south of their location, north of the airport."

"Thirty northwest, caught between a ravine and bad guys, and forty north, surrounded and taking heavy fire," Coop repeated. "South?"

"Nothing."

"Home base?"

"I keep trying, but nothing is getting out or coming in," the PFC replied.

Coop started to reply when a buzz in his earbuds stopped him. He cupped his hands over both ears.

"This is Shooter One. Do you copy?" he asked the buzz, hoping it represented someone live on the other end.

He gave his spotter a questioning look, and received a head shake in reply.

Whoever reached Cooper, had not been heard by Ivanov. That should not have been possible, but Jammers were never perfect. They often created anomalies for communications tech.

This anomaly became a scratchy male voice.

"This is Sixth Fleet communications control, Sardinia. We are receiving broken transmissions, over."

"Sixth Fleet, I am with Can-Am Force Recon. Location, Boudiaf air and spaceport facilities in Constantine, Algeria. I have soldiers pinned down in multiple locations by unexpected superior numbers. I need air support as quick as it can get here."

Static and reverb almost made Coop remove the earpiece. He resisted, fearful of doing anything resulting in loss of the shaky connection.

"Sixth, please repeat."

"Sorry, Shooter one," came the response. More of a gargle than garbled. "All air assets are currently engaged. We have nothing available. Can you retreat? Over."

"Negative. One group is backed against a ravine. One group is caught beneath a highway overpass, taking heavy fire. I have another group unaccounted. Can you pass intel to Can-Am HQ Tunis? We have bad coms."

No reply. No static. Dead air.

"Sixth Fleet? They're gone," he told Ivanov. "Even if they reach Tunis, our guys will be toast before anyone arrives to help."

"What's the plan, Coop? I'm sure as hell not bugging out."

"Do you realize how difficult life is going to be when you get your third stripe?" Coop asked. "You'll be Sarge Serg."

The spotter dropped his optics and let his forehead sink to the sand.

"Only you think of things like that at times like this," he said. "Do you ever get rattled?"

"Whatever is jamming the signals has to be damn powerful," Coop said. "It's capable of squelching point-to-point and sat-rad communications. It isn't perfect, but effective. We need to find it and take it out. If we can improve coms, we can work out a strategy with the teams and find the South group."

"Any clue what to look for?"

"It will be up high, and need to either be flat and round, or on a swivel to effect an area this large," Coop answered. "A swivel would explain why we have intermittent access."

"It could be up on a mountain, or on top of a building somewhere is the city," Ivanov complained.

"Anything so important will be close to the commander, and the commander is at the spaceport. The eastern sky is getting lighter, Serg. Use your optics to check the top of every structure around the port facilities."

Ivanov adjusted his optical scanners, and began a grid search of the airport. Coop recovered his gunny sack. He extracted a tool and used it to remove the barrel of his rifle. He pulled a longer, wider bore barrel from the sack, and set to work attaching it to the stock. By the time he completed all the adjustments, Ivanov had located the suspected jammer.

"When did we get a cannon?" the former Russian soldier asked.

"The original piece belonged to my great grandfather. My Dad had the parts re-milled so it could be mounted on a standard frame. What did you find?" Coop asked back.

"A dish on top of an old-fashion control tower, making three hundred-sixty rotations slowly. Location is fifty-yards east and center to the main runway."

"Distance?"

"Two thousand six-hundred forty-three meters," came the response. "We need to get closer for you to have a chance of taking out any operators."

"Closer means the potential of being seen before we can make a shot," Coop said. "It also means moving to a lower elevation. From the top of this hill to the top of the tower, how much elevation change?"

Ivanov consulted his optics, and replied, "Twenty-one feet."

Coop extended the carbon tripods and settled the weapon on the crest of the hill.

He opened the chamber, and pulled a bullet from the gunny sack's side pouch.

"Mother Mary of God, Coop," the private exclaimed. "That's a fucking artillery shell."

"2,400 grains of lead and 240 grains of smokeless powder," Coop replied, placing the mammoth bullet into the slide chamber. "A .905 caliber capable of 2,100 feet per second."

"Your normal load is two-hundred grains of lead. What kind of kick is that thing got?"

"277 foot-pounds. I've modified the frame with additional absorption, and added extra venting to allow more gas to escape. It's still going to kick like a mule, but a smaller mule."

"So a jackass," Ivanov quipped.

"Call the target, Spotter."

"You have distance and elevation. Forty-eight percent humidity, and zero wind. No mirage effects on the board. I have no idea what a .905 does over distance, so the shot is yours. Hit or miss. I still don't see anyone to target."

What the shot did was contact the base of the jammer disc. The force of impact shattered the steel and carbon into shards. Eight French mercenaries operating and protecting the equipment died from shrapnel. Ivanov watched in amazement as the entire thirty-foot circumference dish tilted. Gravity took control and the jammer fell from the top of the ancient control tower.

"Holy Mother, Coop. Coop?"

The recoil dislocated Cooper's shoulder. The rifle lay to his right side. He held his right arm across his chest. Ivanov had to put it back in the socket.

"Didn't expect that," Coop said a few minutes later, needing the time to bring the pain under control. "I don't think I set the barrel properly." He loosened the utility belt at his waist, gingerly lay his hand across the front of his hip, and tightened the belt over the wrist, securing his arm to his side.

"Coop, you just took down a massive electronic jamming station, from over one-and-a-half miles, with a bullet. If I didn't have the optics system video, no one would believe me."

"Can-Am Recon, this is Sixth Fleet pilot nearing Constantine. Can anyone hear me?"

The discernibly female voice spoke in Coop's ear, but Ivanov's reaction indicated he received the same request.

"Pilot, this is Shooter One. Jammer has been destroyed. We have coms. I'll be your eyes on the ground. What do I call you?"

The hesitation lasted long enough, Coop and Ivanov were just starting to worry the French renegades had more than one Jammer.

"Call sign *Orphan*, Shooter One. Where do you need me first?"

SARDINIA
(Sixth Fleet Communication Center)

"Sorry, Shooter one," responded SPC Hadley. "All air assets are currently engaged. We have nothing available. Can you retreat? Over."

"Negative. One group is backed against . . ." and the reply ended. Communications once more interrupted.

"Is there anything we can do?" Rachelle asked the coms operator. Tentative light gave color to the eastern horizon when Rachelle requested Hadley's attention. She had no official qualifications, certainly no Fleet certifications in communications systems, but knew her way around the sophisticated equipment. During busy times, the communications commander used her to listen for random signals. When aviation assets were engaged with multiple missions, the trained, limited availability specialists, like SPC Hadley, needed to concentrate on those messages.

The erratic chatter from North Africa caught her attention. Once she grasped the situation, she asked Hadley for help.

"I'm forwarding copies to Can-Am, Tunis," Specialist Hadley replied. "I don't think they have air capability to reach those guys in time, but maybe."

"He sounded calm," Paré commented.

"Sniper," Hadley responded. "Call sign Shooter One; has to be a sniper. Those guys have no nerves."

The Specialist rolled his chair three-feet to a second monitor station, swiped a couple of requests on a built-in trackpad, and read aloud the result.

"One hundred-twenty Can-Am Ranger special operators sent to Constantine, Algeria to eliminate an estimated two to three-hundred French ex-military. Sounds like their intel sucked. Unexpected numbers probably means more than a thousand."

"Will they get out?"

"Some might. Rangers are tough. If they can make it to open land, they'll disappear into the deserts and mountains. If they are caught without an exit, most are dead or captured."

"The sniper?"

"Crew is probably in a safe place, high enough and far enough away to cover the killing field. They could bug out. But they won't."

"Why not?"

"Rachelle, there is just something not quite sane about snipers and the crew who work with them. They'll lay down cover fire until someone pinpoints their location and lobs a mortar on top of them. Hey, where you going?"

The door closed behind her without a reply.

CONSTANTINE

"Hold, Orphan." Coop turned coms over to Ivanov, pulled the extended rifle up, and opened his scope. While Cooper took visuals, Ivanov made contact with the two groups under fire.

"The guys at the ravine have cover," he told Coop. "They're pinned, but they can keep their heads down. They have enough firepower to keep the Frenchies back.

"The two groups under the bridge are getting hammered. Coop, my portable lase-designator isn't going to be able to pinpoint targets at either location accurately from this distance."

"Let me have your laser rifle," Coop said, placing the gunpowder weapon down.

"Tell both groups to release green smoke."

He turned his attention back to the flyer.

"Orphan, do you copy?"

"Copy. I'm two-minutes out and hot."

Any girl with a jet and missiles is most definitely hot, he thought to himself. Aloud, he said, "Green smoke will be good guys. Two groups. One north of the space port under a highway overpass. Second group northwest caught in a ravine. Highway bridge is priority. We're too far away to lase the bad guys. I'm going to use a shoulder-fire laser rifle to light the spots you need to hit. Can you target on my shots?"

"Don't know until we try, Shooter One. Beginning my run; fire away."

Ivanov's laser rifle did not come with a scope. It was a defensive weapon designed to protect the sniper crew in case of detection. Coop relied on remembering what he saw with the sniper-scope earlier.

The laser rifle stock set against his left shoulder, weapon supported across his freed damaged right arm. He fired four times, left to right, aiming center of where he recalled mercenary groups positioned and firing on the encircled Can-Am Rangers.

The sniper crew neither heard nor saw the fighter, but hell rained down on the four marks Coop hit.

"Holy shit and my Mother is a whore," the Russian said. He said it twice. The first time in English, followed by Russian for emphasis. "I don't know which is more unbelievable. You hitting targets from this distance, with a fucking unreliable laser rifle, left handed, or a pilot dropping missiles on the exact spots without a guidance system."

Laser fire from near the airfield erupted into the dim sky of night-morning. Two mobile anti-aircraft units attempting to hit the fast-moving fighter.

Coop did not hesitate. He trained the laser rifle on the two enemy sites, and triggered bursts back and forth, trying to disrupt the gun crews.

One of the mobile units turned to face his position, attempting to use the surface-to-air weapon to target and eliminate the threat he posed.

Two missiles streaked in from the West. One for each gun. The incoming missiles eradicated the weapon systems, and everything around them.

"Orphan, are you ready for the ravine?"

"Waiting on you Shooter One, but I did get a look when I flew over. Your guys are close to the bogies. I'll have to use my mini-gun. Can you set a pattern from north to south?"

"Say when."

"When."

Coop fired seven times into the smaller team positions established by the renegades along a highland east of the ravine.

With the sun rising over the horizon, rays of light cleared the mountains east of Constantine. Coop and Ivanov could see the Can-Am fighter as it flew from the North, above the city skyline. The belly of the aircraft skimmed feet above the tallest rooftops.

Twenty-caliber death and destruction tore into the ground, beginning from the spot furtherest the sniper crew's location, moving south, through all seven enemy positions. To get to the ground, they had to pass through a lot of bodies.

"North team commander says they are wiping up the leftovers from Orphan's missiles," Ivanov reported. "They have a few mercenaries north of the overpass, but nothing they can't handle. Team West has exited the ravine. The few bad guys left are surrendering."

"South?" Coop asked. "Have we heard anything from the group there?"

"Negative. Jammer is gone, but still no contact. Com systems must all be off-line. Dead, or damaged during the firefight," the spotter surmised. "Individual coms may not have enough power to reach beyond their immediate field."

"Orphan, this is Shooter One. Can you recon south of the airport? We're missing a group of thirty Rangers. No contact in hours, and no set location other than south of the airfield."

"On it, Shooter One."

The fighter, an older US Navy stealth in-atmosphere superjet called a Night Eagle, crossed from the West, low to the deck, and headed south. The black and dark grey plane, flying now below mach, created little sound as it passed.

"Shooter One?"

"Copy, Orphan."

"Your people are in a wadi surrounded by a couple of hundred bad guys. They're taking heavy fire, including lasers. I see a transport-mounted jammer that's causing the interference with coms. More importantly, light artillery is being positioned. If they range in, no way anyone gets out of that ditch."

"Anything you can do, Orphan?"

"I used all six missiles. I'm almost empty on the last gun-pull. Lasers aren't very accurate for air-to-surface, but I don't seem to have another choice. How fast can your other groups get three-miles south of the airport?"

"Spotter is on the horn. Reports both groups headed your way, but forty-minutes minimum," Coop relayed. He and Ivanov were already setting a quick pace headed southeast. Slowed by his damaged arm, they could still get within firing range in a third the time needed by the other groups.

"I'll do what I can. Orphan out."

The sniper crew heard the battle long before getting to a high spot where they could see. Topping a hill, both came to a jarring, jaw-dropping stop.

"I got nothing," Ivanov said. An amazing admission from a man prideful in his ability to find a curse for any occasion.

The Night Eagle employed hover thrusters to remain steady above a desert wadi.

They could barely make out Rangers huddled under rocks and overhangs, heads down as the wash from the thrusters churned sand, dirt, and rocks into the air. The cloud of debris helped hide them from enemy guns.

At the same time, the ship rotated in a slow circle, the pilot firing laser bursts to keep French ex-army soldiers from advancing on the Rangers caught in the wadi.

Projectiles pinged off the armored ship, with an occasional laser burst singeing the Navy paint job, but not penetrating the reinforced airframe.

The Russian tapped Coop on the left shoulder, and pointed to the Northeast. A half-mile from the Rangers and Night Eagle, the mercenaries were setting up a heavy mortar.

Neither needed to say it out loud. With the fighter stationary, a mortar round would cause a lot of damage. It might not destroy the ship, but it would bring it down. A shell impacting near the cockpit would take out the pilot.

Coop handed the laser rifle back to Ivanov, and pulled the sniper rifle out of the long gunny sack the Russian carried on cross-country run.

"You can't switch the barrel with your arm screwed up, and you ain't got the time anyway," the PFC said, watching his younger superior lift the weapon out left handed.

"For a descendant of the great Russian poet Vyacheslav Ivanovich Ivanov, you use the word *'ai'nt'* a lot. Lie down," Coop ordered.

Serg did not bother to argue. He dropped belly down on the hilltop. Coop placed the now-folded gunny sack across the prone man's back, The weight of the barrel soon rested atop the cloth.

"Damn. That thing's heavier than it looks, and it looks like it weighs a ton."

"Shut up. When I tell you, take a deep five-second breath, then let about half out using a three-count, and don't move. They're about to fire the mortar."

Less than five-seconds later: "Take your breath."

Recalling how loud the first shot used to destroy the big jammer rumbled, the Russian cupped his ears as he took a breath. The boom, followed by the weight removed from his back, brought agony and relief.

Too interested in observing the result of the .905, he ignored the ringing in his ears.

"Damn, Coop. You hit the fucking shell at the same time they fired it."

The blast, muted due to his hearing temporarily disrupted by the rifle's retort, must have been loud. The result of the explosion left total devastation. Nothing within one-hundred yards of the artillery piece stood. The blast crater and surrounding damage could only have occurred due to the deto-nation of the mortar shell.

He turned to congratulate his partner and experienced his next heart-stopping moment.

The .905's recoil knocked the young NCO backward. Judging from the angle of his arm, the kick-back dislocate the left shoulder. Luckily SPC Cooper lay unconscious, so the pain was under control.

TUNIS, TUNISIA
(Two Days Later)

Sergeant Daniel Cooper sat upright in his hospital bed.

Reinforcements arrived from Tunis, but they arrived to find Constantine under control of the surviving Can-Am Rangers.

The two other groups converged on the wadi. The wither-ing laser fire from the Night Eagle, the aftermath of the mor-tar explosion, and the loss of so many other assets resulted in a short skirmish, followed by the French laying down weapons and raising hands.

Ivanov informed the pilot Sniper was down, but okay. He watched the outdated Navy fighter disappear into the morn-ing sun, headed home to Sardinia.

"You look like shit, Coop," Ivanov said. He procured Coop's lunch, sat on the nurse's stool he wheeled in from the hallway, and began eating.

"At least my looks are temporary," he quipped. "You, on the other hand, are stuck with ugly for life."

The Russian would have replied, but decided eating pro-vided a better use for his smart mouth.

"How many did we lose?" Coop asked.

That made his visitor place the tray back on the stand.

"Half," he replied. "Would have been a total cluster fuck if Orphan hadn't shown up. Speaking of, you don't know the rest of the story."

"Nurse told me reinforcements from Tunis teamed up with the special operators still standing and finished the mission," Coop replied. "Took the space port, swept the bridges, and collected the remaining ex-armée de terre deserters."

"Not the most interesting thing," Ivanov said. "Not even close. Turns out Orphan is a civilian. She stole a Navy Night Eagle to save our asses."

Coop sat up, grimaced, and leaned back quickly. The pain meds failing to keep pace with the double dislocated shoulders. "Give me the whole story, Serg. Don't make me ask."

Ivanov recounted the rumor he heard from an SPCl assigned to the Tunis Command Center.

"A civilian, a woman, the daughter of an MIA Navy pilot, donated her time to help around the Sixth Fleet since the relocation to Sardinia. She was helping out in the com center and overheard our request for air cover. When Sixth responded with a 'no-can-do,' she commandeered the Night Eagle. The old fighter was kept armed, fueled, and ready in case of an emergency. They stashed it in a make-shift hangar at the end of a city street. Scuttlebutt says Sixth maintains a couple of hold-out fighters, hidden around the docks in case they ever run out of carrier-based assets."

Ivanov, his recitation proving his lineage to the twentieth-century playwright, wheeled the nurse's stool closer to the bed. Though no one else was near enough to hear him had he shouted, he delivered the next information quietly.

"Orphan, real name Rachelle Paré, opened the hangar doors, drove the fucking Eagle down the street, and took off. She radioed control her plan after she cleared the island."

"Paré?" Coop asked.

Serg scooted back a foot, and resumed at a normal volume.

"Father was a French-Canadian businessman working in Naples while her mother, US citizen and Navy pilot, was assigned Sixth Fleet," Ivanov replied, understanding the one-word question. Time together under the conditions the sniper crew operated led to a great deal of simpatico.

"Your contact seems to have heard a lot. What will they do to her?"

"Good news. She can't be courtmartialed," Serg said. He retrieved the food tray, his appetite returning.

"If General Durand [Commander of the Can-Am North African Army] has his way, she'll get a medal. He already told Admiral Murphy she's welcome to come fly Army fighters."

"Anything else I should know about?"

"I'm getting promoted to SPC, and can expect a Bronze Star. For valorous action in the face of the enemy," he answered. "Ain't much of an honor. They said I had to stay on crew with you."

"Congratulations anyway, Serg," Coop said. A smile helped ease a tiny bit of the pain.

The Russian finished a mouthful of warm jell-o before saying, "You get a Silver Star and a stripe, Sergeant."

"Okay, Serg. Why so glum about the medals and promotions?"

"Fucking classified mission. We can't tell anyone." He looked at his friend, closer than a brother, and added, "Who the fuck wants a medal if you can't use it to get laid?"

SARDINIA
(One Week Later)

"Well, well, it's the felon who fell into a load of shit, and came out smellin' like a hero." NFO Turner Irving stood with hands on hips, feet spread, and face twisted in a smile.

"That is the most convoluted thing I have ever heard, Sir," Paré said. She stood in front of the training officer, dressed in an official Sixth Fleet Can-Am Naval-Air flight suit, complete with ensign rank and name patch.

"Yea, well now hear this, Ensign Paré. The state of the Navy must be one of extreme disrepair if the Admiral of the Sixth Fleet is willing to ask the Prime Minister of the Can-Am alliance for a special dispensation to give a civilian, non-military cadet, wet-behind-the-ears, skinny, twenty-something a commission, and assignment to Flight Training School." All said without pause or breath.

"She's a bit more than that, NFO."

Irving snapped to attention a wink quicker than Rachelle.

Admiral Murphy appeared from around the corner of the hangar wherein the borrowed Night Eagle again resided.

"She's the only Can-Am service member, hell, the only person I have ever heard of to receive a military medal for bravery in battle, before officially being a member of the military."

Rachelle broke protocol, dropping out of attention with wide, questioning eyes, and a "Sir?"

"Both of you, at ease," The Admiral ordered. "The PM received video from over a dozen cameras attached to the SO company sent to Constantine. She watched your actions from a lot of viewpoints. Every angle proved you saved a lot of lives, Toni."

She did not correct his use of her 'former' name.

"We can't have an official ceremony, because it was a classified mission," he said. Then continued in a hushed voice. "We do not need the world to know you stole a government aircraft."

He returned to his normal, slightly gruff tone.

"I don't have an actual medal yet, anyhow. But for the record, Antoniette Rachelle Paré, you are hereby awarded the Can-Am Navy's Flying Cross, earned for demonstrating extreme bravery during battle."

The new ENS Paré excused herself to attend her first official squadron meeting.

Lifted spirits evident in the way she glided across the pavement.

"Has anyone told her how close she came to not coming home?" NFO Irving asked the Admiral.

"Not that I'm aware," Murphy replied. "We'll leave it that way, Ty. Sooner or later she'll find out a grunt on the ground saved her ass with a one-in-a-million shot. By then it will just be a footnote. Let her have her day. She earned it."

End

THE RAID AT AJEJ

I wrote this short story at the same time I was writing CONTACT AND CONFLICT. The protagonist in the Space Fleet Sagas, Daniel Marcel Cooper comes with a complex history, but a fairly straight-forward personality. I needed Ajej to help me understand him better.
DF

The North African sun, hotter, brighter, and more relentless than other versions of the same star, dominated the deep blue sky draped over Tunisia. With the sun directly overhead, the five NCO's barely cast shadows.

Gabés, a city of 40,000 following the pandemic's seventy-five percent death rate. Located on the Mediterranean Sea, residents took advantage of a natural harbor and cooling breezes. The city maintained an important oil refinery, and several concrete factories still operated. Growth required a sturdy base, and no one had yet discovered a better product than concrete and cement to build upon.

The ancient city grew in a unique location where ocean, mountain, and desert came together at an ancient oasis. A natural location for travelers to embark on new adventures.

The Can-Am Army established a camp west of the urban center because the local provided access to North Africa by road, rail, sea, and an airport able to handle anything military from helio-hover craft to exotic jets. The tarmac could accept space-worthy shuttle craft, though most landed in the capital of Tunis, and the headquarters of the Can-Am North African Army.

Sergeant First Class Anthony Bellanova called the other four sergeants to an emergency meeting outside the main barracks. These men led the five rifle squads under his command. The Army's responsibilities as part of the effort to unify the planet meant emergency meetings became the norm, not the exception.

"We got us a situation, and a mission," Bellanova informed his three-stripers. "Thirty girls, ages eight to fourteen, were kidnapped from their school in Tataouine. The kidnappers were id'ed as Allah's Fist. HQ-Tunis says we are the nearest garrison with the right assets, so we get the locate-and-rescue order."

Tataouine was once famous because a long time ago, in a world before the oceans rose and the pandemic killed half the population, a series of movies about space rebels fighting an oppressive empire filmed in the desert around the city for background. The director liked the name, *Tataouine*, and used it for the name of the home-world of the movie hero.

"We're taking four rifle squads, some brass for show, and we're gonna get 'em back," Sgt. Bellanova informed them.

A rifle squad consisted of two teams of four, with a sergeant in command. Nine team members times four squads equalled thirty-six soldiers.

"Search and rescue," said a young man in desert-camo BDU, stained from sweat, and wrinkled from being slept in. The bill of his cap curved to help protect his vision from the bright light. Raybans beneath the bill, and a non-regulation scruffy beard beneath the glasses. "Why the brass?"

Sgt. Daniel Marcel Cooper, at only twenty-one years of age, was senior NCO below Bellanova.

One byproduct of the high death rate following the Chinese bio-contagion designed for population control mutated into a global pandemic, was a younger population. Older people proved less resistant, and less likely to move to safer areas. Militaries lost seasoned officers and NCOs. The unification battles following the distribution of the cure required command-level ranks be filled, and some reached those higher rank faster than deserved.

In Cooper's case, no one thought that. Involved with a number of difficult situations since he enlisted at eighteen, his performance record described a cool, capable, and competent operator.

He now commanded eight soldiers; two corporals, and six PFC's. People who appreciated his attention to detail, and his relaxed personality. He told you what to do, and expected you to do it. Fail to obey once, and he explained why you needed to do your job. He took the time to make it clear why he wanted something done his way. Screw up twice, and he kicked your ass, be-damn regulations.

"They ain't high-value targets, but you know damn well media people will get wind of the snatch," Bellanova replied. "Where there's a chance of publicity, you get a natural attraction of brass," he quipped.

"You got thirty to prep. Get your guys, and get your butts to the motor pool."

Dismissed, Coop, and the other squad leaders, left to round up and prepare their squads.

Bellanova and the four squads arrived at the motor pool,to find six vehicles waiting. Normally a search and rescue ground operation would use as few transports as possible. Maintaining a low profile when traveling through hostile territory important to security. A convoy this size would not go unnoticed.

The lead armored command car doubled as a mobile communication center. It carried Major Ellis Stanford, his driver, and a radio operator. A Captain normally lead this type of operation. The Major's presence deemed it an opportunity for a high-profile moment. A successful mission brought the likelihood of recognition by superiors. Even if the mission failed to locate and recover the kidnapped schoolgirls, he would still get points for trying.

Captain David Marshall, and First Lieutenant Jessica Herman rode in the second armored vehicle in the queue. Both seasoned officers, and both with experience on similar recovery missions in North Africa over the preceding year. Coop had been assigned tasks under both, and had always been comfortable with their orders. A corpsman/medic rode with them and the driver.

Two heavily armored personnel transports followed. Sand-colored camo exteriors, and built to travel off-road across almost any terrain. These battle-busses could deflect small-arms fire, up to shoulder-fired explosive rounds. The special plated material would absorb laser-hits and keep those inside safe. Each bus featured a roof-mounted .50-caliber machine gun. These two vehicles carried the rifle squads, with Second Lt. René LeClaire aboard the first, and Master Sgt. Bellanova in the second.

Another bus-like carrier would be used to ferry the girls home. Armored for protection, but not as heavily as more traditional military vehicles, and without the added machine gun.

Last in line, a new player in the Army's garage. The Recon All-Terrain Transport, gleefully called the RAT.

The RAT carried two soldiers, rode on over-sized all-terrain tires, but had hover capability over short distances. A swivel-mounted laser cannon on the roof, and the remaining space in the van-sized vehicle dedicated to power plants.

Armored, fast on flat surfaces, hooked into satellites for surveillance and real-time visuals, and ugly. This would be its first mission in North Africa. An Army specialist in training, and a civilian trainer crewed the car.

Major Stanford mounted the hood of his command car to address his operators and support people.

"We will travel from Gabés to Medenine on the P1. We will move on to Tataouine using the P19. Both highways remain intact. Sat-Recon shows both are easily passable."

Infrastructures were not a priority after the pandemic hit northern Africa. Besides reducing the population to less than half the original number residing along the Mediterranean, roads, highways, and bridges received no on-going maintenance.

"The AT2 [The RAT's official designation] will be coming with us to give the driver crucial training experience, and test the vehicle under battle conditions."

The Major failed to notice as a number of heads dropped, or gave small side-to-side shakes. S&R missions depended on speed and stealth. Smart planning included anticipating a battle *might* happen. Expecting a battle to happen was asking for trouble.

The trip of eighty miles lasted barely under two hours. The convoy travelled the P1 at speed. The old roadway had never seen a great deal of traffic in the decades before the pandemic. The worn surface showed cracks, but those inside the wide-tire transports hardly felt the bumps.

The RAT would separate from the group for side-trips to test tolerances. The driver asked permission of the Major each time, and received an okay every time.

The six-part convoy bunched closely and moved slowly, through Medenine, a place still worried by gangs.

"The Battle of Medenine during World War II was Erwin Rommel's last engagement in Africa before being replaced as head of the Afrika Korps and called back to Germany. The loss marked the beginning of the end for German forces in North Africa."

Coop sat beside Corporal Robert DePaulo, New Jersey native. Both sat facing forward, feet on the empty bench facing them.

DePaulo asked, "You know that? Who the fuck ever heard of Medenine? Sounds like a drug used to treat some sex disease." DePaulo, nineteen, orphaned when the contagion hit the United States' northeastern shore, dropped out of high school. What he lacked in formal education, he replaced with street smarts. His instincts valuable assets on field missions. Coop trusted the short Italian, and liked him in spite of his crude views on life.

"Good idea to know the area you have to fight in, Bobby," Coop said. "Better idea to study old battles. Might help avoid making the same mistakes the losers made."

"Germans likely lost by not having Italians along to save their butts."

"The Africa Korps included thousands of Italians," Coop said. He watched the shadowed buildings and empty streets pass by. The thick, thin strip of transparent material distorting the world on the far side. "Germany and Italy were allies in World War II."

The convoy passed through the town as the sun moved toward the western horizon. They would reach Tataouine in thirty more minutes.

The road south became more weathered, beaten, and avoiding a pothole only meant hitting another one. The drivers soon stopped trying, allowing the suspensions to do what they could to reduce the shock.

The long escarpment that began south of Medenine, rose and took on a more pronounced shape to their left.

The Major did not bother to stop in Tataouine. Neither to recon the school where the girls' abduction occurred, nor speak with the local police. Intel already pointed to Allah's Fist as the fanatics raiding the school. The small, vicious band of radicals had a history of kidnapping for ransom, and to sell women and girls to fund their jihad. A shortage of females in several regions sparked a surge in sex-trafficking during and after the pandemic.

The group worked with other militant groups, but maintained their own compound in the small village of Ajej, fifteen miles southeast of Tataouine.

This area, the southernmost point in Tunisia, bordered Libya and Algeria. It allowed the band of terrorist easy access for escape, and multiple trade routes for transporting human slaves.

The convoy departed the P19 onto a cracked two-lane road. The escarpment towered to 500-feet at some points. The dessert road cut through sections, placing the convoy between rolling hills of sand, rock, and scruffy vegetation.

The village of Ajej set in a fork in the road in the middle of the desert. One road led to the Libyan border, and the other deeper into the Tunisian desert.

Rocks of all sizes and shapes littered the road, spillage from the hills along both sides of the road to Ajej. Sand drifts spread across the asphalt every few hundred feet. Once well traveled, the artery now partially reclaimed by the bleak terrain.

At sixteen-thirty-four hour, the lead command car pulled onto the side of the road. The caravan stopped in a pass-through where the scarp changed from steep slope high to long cliff, forcing highway engineers a century or more earlier to blast a passageway.

"Where are we?" Private Sanchez asked. Part of Coop's team, the Argentinian, a row behind, knelt on his seat and was trying to see though the narrow portal.

"Five miles from the hot zone," Coop answered.

Neither Sanchez or DePaulo questioned his answer. Their sergeant possessed an uncanny ability to study topography maps and process locations while on the move. Cooper never relied on electronics to operate when you most needed them. One failure at the wrong time could kill you.

"Why stop here?" Sanchez asked Coop.

"The Major probably selected the site because the cliffs provide shade," Coop replied.

Even with the sun half-way to the horizon, the heat remained. The cloudless sky made the force of sunlight brighter. The steep slopes bathed the old road in shadows. If it did not actually make the space cooler, it made it look cooler.

"DePaulo, tell people to keep weapons close," he ordered his second. "I'm not comfortable in this bowl."

The Italian made no comment. Coop's instincts saved his ass a number of times in the recent past, so he hurried down the line, making certain everyone held a weapon at the ready.

The convoy stopped in the middle of a desert, on an open road, and with no line of sight east or west. No satellite overhead to provide imagery until after midnight. The mission's original design called for incursion after dark, when their people had a distinct advantage. At this latitude, in summertime, dusk would arrive in four hours.

Coop noted Bellanova, riding a third seat in the transport's cabin, take a private channel communication. The

Sergeant Major tapped the driver's shoulder, and the side door folded out. Bellanova departed, the door closing behind him.

Sgt. Canfield, leader of the other rifle team aboard the transport with Coop's team, echoed his thoughts.

"If it had been up to me, we would have stayed in Tataouine, gone over the mission plan, prepped, and headed out after dark. We don't have a satellite available for another seven or eight hours. Do you think Stanford is planning on us parking here until then?"

"Don't know the Major well enough to know what he's thinking," Coop replied. "Sanchez, take the fifty-cal seat. See if the top of the bus is higher than the surrounding dunes."

The PFC lowered the roof-mounted ladder and scurried up. He found a seat behind a machine gun placed inside a semi-transparent dome. His feet operated the drive train, and the dome tracked left to right.

"I got nothing, Sarge," he called down. "Bunch of officers out front having tea and biscuits, open road behind us, and sand everywhere."

Major Stanford did not possess field experience. If not for his desire to reach Lt. Colonel, and a reassignment away from North Africa to somewhere, anywhere more civilized, he would not be standing in the heat trying to decide between a more daring, and dangerous, early evening raid versus returning to Tataouine. Going now meant using old intel. Going back meant more hours spent waiting.

After calling the convoy to a halt, he ordered a meeting of the officers and Sergeant Major.

"They could be moving the girls right now," he said to those assembled in front of his command vehicle. "If we wait until we have eyes on the compound, we risk losing them."

"We may have forced them to speed up their plans by parading through cities and towns on the way here," Captain Marshall said. His observation more a comment on the Major's lack of finesse and timing than probable enemy actions.

The first of two RPG's hit while the Major considered his reply to the Captain.

Both officers, two lieutenants, and Bellanova, all standing in front of the forward command vehicle, died. Because the vehicle's doors were left open, the second RPG killed the driver and the communication specialist.

The explosive loads, tenth generation descendants of the original Rocket Propelled Grenades, carried non-nuclear high-yield thermal charges. There would be no bodies to bag, and even the heavily armored transports could be damaged, if not destroyed.

The attack originated from the eastern side of the road, from 300-feet up, atop the cliff opposite the one providing shade.

Soldiers exited the two troop carriers, firing projectile-load rifles and shoulder-fire lasers. Because Sanchez already sat behind the fifty-cal, he sent high-velocity projectiles raking across the top of the scarp.

While most secured cover behind the transports, Cooper grabbed two of his squad, and bolted toward the transporter meant for the girls.

His plan was to circle around the rear of the bus, and onto the easier slope to their rear, eastern side.

Quick reflexes saved him and the two following him.

The RAT, driven by a panicked rookie, rammed into the rear of the transport. Coop pulled up, rotated, and body-slammed the two privates to the ground seconds before the impact. Had he not acted, the three would be hamburger.

The RAT lurched backward. The passenger-side hatch opened, and the civilian tech yelled, "Are you okay?"

Coop screamed at the civvie to close the hatch, but the warning came too late.

The sound of the crash attracted the attention of their attackers, and when the hatch opened, laser-fire rained down on the RAT, slicing into the tech.

The driver was hurt, killed, scared or a combination because the AT2 spun wildly. It finally stopped spinning when the front end buried itself into a sand dune.

"Go," Coop called.

The time spent together in training, and, more importantly, on missions, negated the need for talk. The two riflemen followed without question. Coop ignored the spinning vehicle and ran for the hill. The three up and across a lower section of the escarpment before the RAT's nose hit.

Coop did not turn towards the location of the ambushers, but continued forward, maintaining a bone-jarring pace until the three stopped a good 500-feet into the desert.

Like most fault-produced ranges, the terrain on either side of the raised land proved to be flat.

Staying silent, the three headed north, taking advantage of the flat surface for speed over stealth.

They found two tricked-out dune buggies. The attackers had, most likely, been keeping tabs on the convoy by driving the flatland, hidden by the hills. A quick check to insure no one remained with the vehicles, and they moved onto the slope rising up to a cliff. Four militants fired down on the soldiers hidden behind the transports.

Two spent RPG launchers lay on the ground.

The four enemy combatants, engrossed in their effort to kill the soldiers in front and beneath them, never considered their rear. The three experienced Can-Am regulars required less than two minutes to ambush and eliminate the ambush-ers.

Coop keyed his mike to inform DePaulo.

"Enemy to your east no longer a threat," he told his second. "Dispatch two teams west. Make sure we don't have anyone tracking us on that side."

It took longer to disable the buggies and discard weapons found by tossing them further into the desert, than needed to eliminate the four shooters. Communications gear consisted of short-range com-talkers, and a longer range radio. The radio did not have sat-link, so it was limited to the horizons.

"These four may have radioed their position and the situation. If so, more of their kind are approaching," Coop said. He was thinking out loud, more so than addressing his two soldiers.

"If they took the opportunity to attack because of where we stopped, and were intent on the kill, they might have remained dark. It may be hours before they're missed."

Coop turned, looking in all directions.

"The radio would not reach Ajej from down here, below the escarpment," he said. "Hell, they could be from another group. We might have picked them up along the way."

"How do we know for sure?" PFC Kebede asked.

Coop refocused. The Ethiopian transfer joined his team a few days earlier. This had been her first field test. They lived, the bad guys did not. She passed.

"Without a bad guy to ask, no way to know," he answered.

As soon as they made it down the slope, Cooper, the highest ranking soldier on site, took control. They policed bodies, and body parts, placing what they could gather into bags. Forensics could sort later.

The corpsman from the second vehicle attended to a variety of injuries. Laser burns, bullet holes, and one sprained ankle.

It was necessary to abandon the lead command vehicle. The interior far too damaged by the second RPG to operate.

They did bag the civilian tech. The RAT operator settled enough to disengage the vehicle from the hill. He parked in the middle of the road. Missed by the laser fire slicing his trainer, his vomit mixed in with seared flesh.

One thing about lasers; they cauterized at the same time they killed you. Only a little blood splatter.

Coop ordered everyone aboard once the medic completed his field work. Vehicles turned, and return to Tataouine. Coop now in Marshall's seat, riding point in the remaining command car.

They stopped on the outskirts of the ancient city. Coop reconnoitered on foot while the fifty-calibers on top of the buses stood watch. Thirty-minutes later he directed the four remaining vehicles behind an adobe wall once used to protect a villa's courtyard. He contact Major Stanford's superior, General Brendan Durand in Tunis, but not until after setting pickets.

The coms operator at Can-Am North Africa HQ decided to argue about putting him through to the General.

"Soldier, I have four dead officers, a Sergeant Major, and a civilian tech in body bags. The mission was ordered by General Durand. If you want to inform him later you decided not to put this call through, that's your decision. He can only have you shot once."

General Durant, head of the Can-Am presence in North Africa, came on within two minutes. Because North Africa was designated a Unified Combatant Command, Durant was a four-star, and commanded every ground, sea, and air unit in the region.

"Sit-rep, Cooper," he demanded. Even though Cooper was a lowly three-striper, he had previously met General Durand. Both times to receive medals.

"Ambushed on the road to Ajej. Major Stanford, Cpt. Marshall, Lt.s Herman, and LeClaire, and Master Sergeant Bellanova all KIA by RPG. One driver, one specialist, and the civilian AT2 trainer also KIA. I have six soldiers wounded, including a squad leader. Five are ambulatory, one out. I have thirty-one fully capable operators, plus four drivers. I also have a specialist learning how to operate an AT2 without supervision."

"The wounded?" Durand asked. Recognizing the real priorities in a battle is the first sign of a good superior officer.

"The medic says everyone is stable. None critical. The walking wounded can still handle weapons."

"You don't want to scrub the mission, do you?" Durand half asked, half commented.

"Still thirty girls out here, General. We have decent intel where they are tonight, but in the morning, it's a quick trip to Libya or Algeria. We'll never get them back after they move."Cooper let the statement stand.

"You do not know the number of enemy combatants."

"Didn't know the number before. We usually don't until we're toe-to-toe."

"Let me get communications on the line, and you find a witness," he told Cooper. The line turned to dead air.

Cooper called for Corporal Robert DePaulo, and told him to wait.

"Sgt. Cooper, are you there?" Coop switched his phone to speaker to allow DePaulo to hear.

"I'm on, General. Cpl. DePaulo is present," Coop replied.

"Tech Specialist Peterson, are you on line?" the General asked.

"Coms on line," came the immediate reply.

"Sgt. Daniel Cooper, under my authority as General of Can-Am forces in North Africa, and due to the unique situation which occurred during a battlefield operation, I hereby assign you the rank of First Lieutenant. Specialist Charneau, and Cpl. DePaulo, did you hear, and do you understand the order?"

Both confirmed the battlefield promotion of Sgt. Cooper to Second Lt. Cooper. Charneau would type the order, and send it to admin for filing. DePaulo's responsibility involved confirming the promotion to the other soldiers in the field.

"Lt. Cooper, if you believe the personnel you have can complete the mission, then I expect you to go find, free, and return those girls. If, at any time, you decide the risks outweigh the rewards, you are to abort and return to Gabés. I expect to be kept in the loop, Lieutenant."

"Yes, sir. Cooper, out." The newly minted lieutenant began his first assignment as the officer in charge.

"Stand still." a smiling DePaulo told him. He produced a black marker, and deftly drew the bar insignia of a second lieutenant on the collars of Coop's shirt. The shorter Italian-American stepped back, gave a sharp salute, and said, "I gotta go tell the troops." He left Lt. Cooper to ponder his new situation.

Thirty-minutes later, Coop's entire team, including walking wounded, circled him. The meeting protected within the walls of the old courtyard, and the soldiers on guard duty.

"We wait here until Twenty-three hundred hours," Lt. Cooper informed them. "An orbital satellite with optics and heat sensors passes overhead at midnight. We'll have access for a limited window, and I expect us to be on target by midnight to take advantage of that window.

"When we leave, we travel into Tataouine. The convoy will take the turn onto A-19 north. If the enemy has eyes on us, I want them to report we decided to trash the rescue. At the northern end of the city, there is an unpaved route that bends east and south on the far side of the escarpment. It passes a couple of desert farms, and connects to the road north of Ajej, south of where we were ambushed."

Coop hesitated a moment. He considered opening the meeting to discussion, and quickly decided he had to act like the officer in charge. His command, his plan.

"From the moment we leave the A-19, we go stealth. All vehicles employ infrared headlights. Drivers use your optics, and engage hyper-quiet mode on all engines."

Using the side of a transport vehicle, Coop used a piece of chalk to diagram the mission old-school style. No electronic pads, high-def screens, or sharing data. Just a bunch of grunts on the ground.

"The suspected compound for Allah's Fist is on the southern side of Ajej where the road forks. Intel described the compound with a multi-story house, a barn and attached corral, another large building that could be a barracks, and a hut on stilts, which is most likely a watchtower.

"We will leave the vehicles north of Ajej, and approach the compound on foot. A three mile jog in the dark. Once on site, I want reconfirmation of the layout. Make sure it is a force location, and not a mom-and-pop farm. When we know the location is hot, we uplink to the satellite, and finalize insertion tactics based on the latest intel.

"Questions?" No one spoke.

"Grab something to eat, and get rest. Sgt. Clayton will assign watch rotations. Everyone in the saddle at twenty-three hundred."

The meeting went to Sgt. Clayton, who made the assignments for watch stations and patrols.

At twenty-three-hundred local time, the convoy departed the courtyard, and made its way through the small city. At the intersection of A-19 and the old farm road, they switched to infrared for visual and stealth-drive on engines.

They arrived north of Ajej at twenty-three-thirty-two (11:32pm).

The vehicles left the paved road, taking a gentle slope up and over a lower hillock. Coop brought them to a halt at the foot of the hill. He ordered the five wounded warriors and four drivers remain as rear guard, with Squad Leader, Sgt. Hammonds in charge. They hoisted soldiers with leg wounds into the gun-ports atop the armored buses. Their wounds would not prevent them from handling the .50-caliber machine guns.

He considered ordering one or two rifle teams to remain with them, but decided he needed the fire power. The vehicles and weapons offered a lot of protection for the walking wounded and drivers.

Finally, he pulled the specialist assigned the AT2 aside. He had taken the time to speak with the shaken specialist at the villa courtyard, learn his name, and make sure he was still capable of performing his tasks. He did not have the time then, or now to coddle the young man.

"Corporal Fuhrman, point your RAT at the hill we just came over. Turn on every sensor the vehicle has and monitor the ridge behind this position. You will warn Sgt. Hammonds if anything appears, and you will, if needed, protect his six."

Fuhrman, not a seasoned field operator, but a tech specialist, appreciated the tone of his new commander. He also appreciated not being asked, but told. It meant Coop had confidence he could and would do the job assigned.

"Yes, sir," he replied. Eyes up, head up.

Thirty-three soldiers, including the medic, made the jog to the compound. Using GPS to keep them on track, it took thirty minutes to reach a hillock overlooking the suspected Allah's Fist training center. They could normally run eight-minute miles, but the softer sand, undulating dunes, and darkness slowed them.

The satellite pinged available in Coop's earpiece by the time they reached the overlook, but he did not try to establish contact. First, they used advanced night vision optics with heat-sig overlays to surveil the local terrain and compound layout.

Their position provided elevation for a visual confirmation on house, barracks, barn, corral, and watchtower. They revealed a field, with obstacle course added, for training. Cooper spotted two people on the porch of the house when one lit a cigarette. Bad field craft.DePaulo elbowed him, pointed towards the barn, and raised four fingers. Cooper confirmed four militants walking guard around the barn and corral. A sliver of light leaked from inside the barn, escaping though the front doors left ajar.

A group of vehicles sat parked beside the barn, on the same side as Cooper's team. Heat-sensitive optics indicated all engines cold. No guards deployed.

The moon, three-quarters full, sat high in the cloudless night sky. Bright enough, the guards did not require additional light. Bright enough to make an approach difficult, as well. Normal night-incursion missions opted for moonless nights. Time-sensitive jobs played the hand dealt.

The watchtower sat dark, but had to be considered a danger. A yellow-tint light shone in the back of the first floor of the farmhouse. Probably the kitchen. A second dim glow emanated from a room on the second floor.

Coop had seen enough to confirm their basic intel remained correct, and the compound inhabitants not mom and pop farmers. He scurried down to the hillock's base, and pulled his field tablet from his backpack. He did not chance the soft light of the screen being noticed. A fingerprint scan, followed by an anti-clockwise loop to confirm his authority, and the screen lit a soft green. He tapped an icon, and instantly engaged the spy satellite overhead.

He checked different views, formats, and angles before putting the tablet to sleep. He motioned for DePaulo, and the two remaining sergeants.

"Positive on six guards. Four at the barn, and two outside the house. We have a couple of mixed signatures inside the barn. Could be people, could be animals. The corral is filled with live bodies. I'm guessing that's where they have the girls.

"Nothing from the watchtower. The barrack appears filled. Heat signatures evenly spaced, so probable targets asleep in bunks. I counted twenty-three. The house is too insulated for good readings. Could be one bogie inside, or might be a dozen.

"Clayton [Sgt], you have your full squad, so I want you set up around the barracks. Take the six left from Hammonds' teams. Make sure all four sides are covered. If anyone tries to come out the doors or windows, take them out. You are designated *TEAM GREEN*.

"DePaulo, Cantor, Lewiston, Kebede, and I will take out the barn guards. We are *TEAM ONE*. Once they are down, Canfield (Sgt.) will bring the remaining soldiers in to keep the girls quiet, and safe. Canfield is *TEAM BEAR*."

Assigning each team a designation of color, number, or animal kept the chances of a misunderstanding at a minimum.

Coop continued the field plan.

"After Canfield has control of the corral, Team One will clear the barn. If we still haven't woken the barracks, the five of us will clear the house. The four soldiers with TEAM BEAR from my original squad will cover our six.

"Corpsman Jeremy will remain on the hill to monitor the view from the satellite. If anyone enters from the surrounding area, he'll give us an SOS beep on the open channel. Questions?"

"What happens when all hell breaks loose?" Sgt. Clayton asked, half kidding, but mostly serious.

"We protect the girls," Coop replied. "That's the mission. Eliminate any threat."

With no more questions, the two squad leaders left to gather their newly blended teams. DePaulo went to round up Corporals Tony Cantor and Tanika Lewiston and Specialist Senait Kebede.

Cantor and Lewiston were the two top hand-to-hand fighters in all of the rifle teams; just a hair behind Cooper and DePaulo. They both excelled at in-close knife work. Each accurate with laser pistol, shoulder fired laser, and the older, but often more reliable, projectile weapons. Kebede recently joined the squad, but had proven reliable to this point. Other than Kebede, the other four successfully worked together several times in the past year to silently, and quickly clear open and closed spaces of bad guys.

Coop sat cross-legged on the ground. The four others stood behind, looking over his shoulders at the field pad screen. He tapped an enemy guard on patrol, and said, "De-Paulo." Next guard to Cantor, and one to Lewiston. He was responsible for number four.

"Kebede, watch our backs. Anything and everything else is your responsibility."

He keyed his mike to open all channels.

"Every time you hear a single audio tap, it will confirm a kill. Clayton, take up positions around the barracks. Canfield, on the fourth tap, move in to the corral."

He ordered Sgt. Canfield to send the three females on his newly formed team into the coral first. He hoped their presence would calm and quiet the girls more quickly. A bunch of screaming teenage girls would send the mission down a dangerous path.

Coop dispatched Doc (Corpsman Jeremy), with the field pad, to the top of the hillock. He and his rifle team went up with the medic, leaving him on the crest as they crawled down the side facing the compound. At the bottom, they crab walked to positions. Each special operator fingered their mike a quick double-tap, 'beep-beep,' to confirm they were in place and ready. Following the fourth confirmation, he gave three quick taps for the go-ahead signal.

Within two minutes, everyone on the mission heard one, then two, a third, and finally a fourth "beep," indicating all four guards were down — and down meant dead.

Clayton's team had positions around the barracks where suspected militants slept. They prepared to rain fire down on the structure if needed.

Canfield's team, lead by the female soldiers, entered the corral through the gate. Cooper, and his squad members waited, having cleared the way. The five trained weapons on the partially open barn door. The nine remaining soldiers spread out around the corral, which had been reinforced with concertina wire to prevent the girls from escaping. The female team members began waking girls. Each placed a hand over a mouth, letting them see a woman held them. Next, they showed them the Can-Am flag insignia normally Velcroed on their left shoulder, but removed during stealth operations.

Those girls helped wake others, using the international symbol for quiet - index finger to the lips - until everyone was awake and aware of the soldiers now protecting them.

One of the older girls took Cpl. Melissa Bynes' hand, pulled her close, and whispered. Bynes quickly found Cooper.

"Sarge, sorry, I mean, Lieutenant, one of the girls says three other girls were taken away. Two in the barn, and one in the house."

Coop nodded, and motioned for TEAM ONE to join him, and Bynes.

First, he moved them away from the entrance. He turned to Bynes, pointed at the barn door, and pretended to fire a gun with his right index finger. She would watch the door, and shoot anyone not them who came out.

His back to the barn, Coop whispered, "There are two girls in the barn. Doc says satellite puts heat center, rear, but indistinct. Not sure who, what, how many or in what condition. DePaulo, do you have oil in your pack?"

"Affirmative," the corporal replied, pulling the backpack off, and swinging it around to get to a pocket. He displayed a tin of lubricating oil. His job now to grease hinges, so the barn door did not squeak an alert when opened.

"DePaulo, and I go left. Lewiston, and Cantor right. Kebede cover center, but stay out of the doorway. Do not make yourself a target. Use pistols with suppressors. No lasers. I don't want us lighting the place up, or catching hay on fire."

With the hinges oiled, Coop slowly opened the doors wider so they could slip inside. Two left, two right, one on knee inside left of doors. Nothing moved. No words of warning, and no one fired at them. It was not difficult to see inside the barn. Near the back of the utility structure, an old-fashion lightbulb hung from a stable wall.

Two girls, early teens, both nude, hung by their wrists from hooks in the ceiling supporting the hayloft. Gagged. Heads down. Sweat-drenched hair hanging in front of their faces. Their toes barely reached the hard dirt floor, with their heels up.

A skinny dark-haired man, with no shirt, and no shoes, was seated against the stable wall. His head tilted back in sleep. Coop waited for everyone to agree the sleeping guard was the only other person present. He moved forward, cat-foot quiet. He grabbed the militant by the hair, turned his head aside, and slit his throat. By turning him, the spray of blood gushed away from Coop. The man's eyes opened wide, and quickly glazed over in death.

With help from the other three, they cut the two girls down, making sure they remained quiet. Discarded clothing lay in bundles on the floor nearby. It took a few minutes to get the girls dressed, their muscles unable to cooperate. It was obvious they could not stand on their own, or walk. De-Paulo picked up one girl, and Cantor the other, taking them out to the corral to join the others. Bynes did not shoot them.

Less than fifteen minutes on mission, and the most important concern, the girls, was in hand. Except for one miss-

ing child. The most difficult task lay ahead. The house needed to be cleared.

DePaulo oiled the hinges of the front door, and tossed the
can to Cantor. With Lewiston, they would go to the rear, and
do the same to the door they assumed opened into the
kitchen. Two beeps announced Cantor and Lewiston were
ready. Cooper gave the answering three quick clicks, and he
and DePaulo entered the front. Coop tracked right. DePaulo
covered left.

The front porch provided line of site to the barn, the
watchtower, and the barracks. Kebede's position allowed her
to watch all three, making sure no one surprised the team
inside.

Cooper heard two puffs from down a hallway, coming
from the rear off the house. There were no other sounds, and
the soft *puff-puff* would not have been heard upstairs. He
and DePaulo cleared the three downstairs rooms at the front
of the house. They slowly entered the kitchen via a swinging
door.

Lewiston stood guard beside the door, his silenced pistol
aimed at their heads as they entered. Cantor stood watch at
the back door. Lewiston lowered the weapon. Coop saw two
dead bad guys laid out on the kitchen floor. The stove was lit,
and a couple off pots of coffee, or tea sat on top. The kitchen
left open so guards on duty could take breaks.

Using hand signals, Cantor was to remain on guard in the
kitchen. Lewiston to follow Coop and DePaulo. Coop took
lead, heading up the stairwell, stepping on the outside of
each riser to lessen the chance of a squeak from an overused
middle section. DePaulo followed, with Lewiston covering
the rear.

The top floor corridor extended from the stairs to a door.Three more doors stood closed on the right. Nothing but wall on the left.

Starting at the first door on the right, Cooper entered a bedroom. He dawned night-vision goggles before entering the house, and other than the short time in the kitchen, kept them on. The green-tinted view showed a form on a double bed. It proved to be a sleeping man. Coop had no qualms about firing a bullet into the back of his head.

The next door was another bedroom, with two men in two single beds. He killed one with a shot to the forehead. The second must have heard the soft puff, but died without discovering what disturbed his rest, a bullet in his right eye.

The next door was a bathroom. It had a light on, but no one inside. DePaulo stayed close behind to cover Coop's six. Lewiston took position at the top of the stairs, so he could cover the corridor and the stairwell.

The final door opened into a large bedroom with a king size bed. A girl, a small girl, lay naked atop the sheets.Her soft sobs interrupted by tiny hiccups as she tried to get air. A big, hairy arm thrown over her, holding her on the bed, also made it difficult for her to breath.

Coop backed out and motioned for Lewiston to join him. DePaulo took her place at the top of the stairs. With the female soldier behind him, he walked to the bed, and placed the silenced pistol's muzzle against the base of the head of the big man lying on his belly. He tensed and woke. He was smart enough to remain quiet.

Coop used his left hand to take the guy's arm off of the girl, and Lewiston hurried to pick her up. The girl so traumatized, she did nothing more than bury her head in Tanika's shoulder, and continued to sob. Lewiston grabbed a small throw from a chair next to the bed to cover the child, and hurried out to join DePaulo. As soon as she cleared the room with the youngster, Coop pulled the trigger.

They joined the others at the corral, and everyone began slowly, and quietly walking back up the hillock to join Doc.

After crossing the ridge-line, Sgt. Canfield took the lead. Using GPS on his chronometer, he led the band of soldiers and schoolgirls towards the transport vehicles. Ten-minutes out, Cooper, on drag, contacted the drivers. He ordered them to move towards them. He did not want the kids to walk the entire three miles in the desert. Plus he had three soldiers carrying girls. On second look, he saw at least another half-dozen being piggy-backed by special ops members.

Following the confirmation by the drivers, he contacted-Clayton with a pre-arranged five clicks on the radio. This let the sergeant know his people could depart and act as rear guard.

While they had been waiting for Coop's team to clear the farmhouse, Clayton had his people wire the five vehicles parked next to the barn with explosives.

As they walked to the vehicle convoy coming silently to meet them, Clayton's team caught up. A minute later they were loading the girls onto the transport bus. The two girls from the barn, and the young girl from the house were placed in the command vehicle with Doc, Tanika, and the driver. Coop and DePaulo would ride on the transport bus as guards.

The convoy reached the paved backroad, and the wounded soldiers on top of the armored cars let loose for a full thirty-seconds with the .50 calibers. The girls had been warned, so no one freaked over the incredibly loud sequence.

Coop watched on his satellite link. He saw the barrack come alive with bodies running around. Some to the barn. More to the house. There was general disarray, until someone obviously took charge. All the glowing bodies moved to the side of the barn, and engines flared red on the screen. Coop tapped an icon, and the screen turned orange, yellow, and red. A few seconds later the sound of the combined explosives detonating reached the convoy.

Without concern regarding the time, Coop contacted the Coms Command Center in Tunis, and asked to be put through to General Durand. After asking politely, and being told no, he proceeded to tell the enlisted man on duty what, exactly, he would do to the man if he did not put is call through immediately, and assured him the General would stand by, and watch as he did it.

Durand answered, and not in a sleepy voice. He had been awake and waiting.

"Lt. Cooper, sir. Mission accomplished. I'm taking the girls to the hospital in Gabés. ETA is two hours. You can let their parents know, and they can meet us there. Cooper, out."

He did not wait for a *good job* from the General. He rode a bus with twenty-seven testaments to a job done well.

END

THE SPACE RANGER PROJECT

A Novelette In The Space Fleet Sagas.

The Space Fleet Sagas novels begin with the launch and maiden voyage of the Space Fleet Patrol and Torpedo battleship, John F. Kennedy; SFPT-109.

In Book One of the series, CONTACT AND CONFLICT, I introduce Captain Daniel Marcel Cooper, the first commander of an Earth-based interstellar capable spaceship. A former US Army soldier, Ranger, Can-Am Ranger, Space Ranger, UEC Naval Pilot, test pilot, and Space-Capable vehicle test pilot.

Seems a strong resumé for one person? Possible only because Coop was re-engineered. During the procedure, a longevity gnome buried in human RNA, was activated.

He appears mid to late-twenties, but is actually in his early fifties when the PT-109 takes flight.

Two other Space Ranger alumni are introduced in CONTACT AND CONFLICT; Elena Caslobos and Anton Gregory.

For the Space Fleet Sagas to work, I needed human characters with meta-human attributes. THE SPACE RANGER PROJECT is a novelette. The format allows me to take you back in the future. Journey thirty-years before first contact with aliens, and twenty years following the discovery of the hidden hangar and alien spaceship on Mars that jump-started Earth's introduction to the rest of the galaxy. The format provides the length to help explain how genetic engineering could occur, and the potential pit-

falls. A length you can consume and digest quickly, allow-ing more time and less energy spent reading the novels.

Once you understand how the Space Ranger Project not only created, but brought together many of the major char-acters to appear and reappear in the Space Fleet Sagas, you will understand the fiber of the series. Humanity does not consist of one type of human, and aliens are not so dif-ferent.
DF

THE SPACE RANGERS PROJECT appeared in OMNI magazine, March: 2017.

The Beginning -

The Spanish Legionnaire raked her fingernails from Coop's shoulders to the middle of his back, leaving a blood trail. It drove Coop deeper into her, which was the point. His weight on his elbows and thighs, and her legs crossed behind his low back. The two fought the coming or-gasms, riding the tide. She arched, her breasts pushing into his chest, groaned, and they came in unison.

He lay on top of her for a long moment, their perspira-tion mingling, the heartbeats coming down together. When she uncrossed her legs, he slipped out and rolled over onto the bed. He lay there, eyes closed. If he watched her breasts rising and falling he would want to go again. This was their third orgasm, though the first to be reached in unison.

"I pray we do not have jump-school tomorrow," Elie said, turning on her side to face him. "The thought of those straps between my legs, and how raw I'm gonna be. Ouch." She laughed, then nuzzled his neck.

"I was just thinking about how the shower is going to sting when the water hits my back."

"You were kind enough to help me wash the sand out of all the little places I could not reach. I will not make fun of you if you cry, when your little scratch gets wet."

"In that case, I guess I can afford a few more scratches."

Before The Beginning -

"This project seems premature. We don't have anything close to what anyone could call a spaceship. The advances in travel between Earth and Mars are remarkable, but a long way from SPACE travel."

At the word *SPACE*, the slender woman with long, tapered fingers, and bright blue fingernails, spread them in the air pantomiming a burst.

Melissa Booth, Canada's representative to the United Earth Council (UEC), and, because Canada and the United States created the UEC, a Board of Governors member, sat in her new chair, in her new office, at the new headquarters for the UEC, north of downtown Toronto.

A man in a rumpled dark-blue suit stood in front of her desk, hands gripping the back of a chair. One of two placed there for guests. Neither of which enticed the over-excited man to sit.

"Advances in the human gnome project have allowed geneticists to isolate a section of gene pairs they named the 'Methuselah Sequence'. Four base pairs of genes within the 25,000 total genes, which create humans. The theory behind the sequence surmises centuries ago, prior to the great flood, humans actually lived for hundreds of years. An environmental shift caused humans to lose longevity, but our DNA, or RNA, or whatever, stored the secret in gnomes, and kept the sequence."

Turner Mattson-Grimes managed the fledgling UEC's Marketing and Public Relations Department. Unifying the planet, following the Eastern Pandemic and the subsequent loss of half of the world's population, remained an on-going challenge. Diplomatic reasoning and military force had been, and were still being used to accomplish the impossible. Mattson-Grimes' responsibilities included finding ways to bring the disparate people of Earth opportunities to bond.

Twenty-four, overweight, under-height, and married to his new job. He attacked disharmony the way special operators attacked bunkers. He was determined to find ways to bring the world together, peacefully.

Governor Booth's responsibilities included managing Mattson-Grimes. Before his ideas reached a Council committee for review, they needed to pass inspection by her.

"Why were scientists looking for ways to extend lifespans?" she asked. "We have problems enough simply keeping people alive."

"It actually happened when we were seeking a cure for the pandemic," Mattson-Grimes explained. "One of those happy mistakes. No one pursued it until after a cure was discovered and dispersed."

"So you have a gene proving humans once lived longer. So?"

The PR director continued his presentation.

"Genetic engineers, working with biochemists, developed artificial enhancement cocktails able to increase strength, speed, bone density and activate self-healing properties. Test animals have shown strength gains of nearly six-fold the average. The animals did not reject the cocktails because the ingredients within them were variations of material already found in natural organic matter. A complex variation, but one a host accepts as normal."

"You have this all memorized, don't you," Booth remarked. She slipped off her dress shoes, and rubbed one foot against the other beneath her desk. Science stuff bored her.

"Of course. All of this is important. A bit boring, but essential. Our science teams want to create super-soldiers. I want to create unity."

"Go on, Turner, but you might consider speeding this up. If you put me to sleep, I doubt you will get the committee excited enough to recommend funding for your project."

"Speaking of funding, the massive amount of time, money, and expertise spent finding a cure for the world-wide pandemic, also resulted in associated research producing a serum potentially capable of providing near immunity against bacterial and viral infections."

He released the back of the chair, standing to his full short height. Time for the icing.

"The final ingredient necessary to make the Space Ranger Project actionable happened this year. Dr. Nathan Trent's team decoded more files located in the Martian hangar. The original files helped scientist understand the engineering and technology used to build the space ship found within the hangar."

"Everyone knows about the flying saucer and Dr. Trent, Turner. What's your final ingredient?"

The short, squat man moved around and wiggled into his chair. This was his closer.

"The latest files hold much more information than just space flight specs. One set has to do with re-engineering humanoid bodies. The data closely parallels the same research currently being done on Earth. And, most importantly, Governor Booth, the files provided the final components for success. The ancient astronauts created an organic gel which is activated by a specific combination of lasers and electricity. Drop a body in the gel, zap it to absorb the necessary elements, and we re-engineer a functional human into a super-human."

Mattson-Grimes finally managed to capture her attention, and made the swelling in her feet inconsequential.

"Really? We can make super-humans?"

He had her. He reeled her in, telling her, "Scientists on Mars and Earth studied the data. They tested the gel on animals with complete success, once the proper use of lasers and electricity was finally achieved." He sat back. Time to replace emotion with reason.

"The only thing they need to add is activating the Methuselah Sequence. They are ninety-nine percent sure they can revive the RNA during the re-engineering process.

"The UEC, hell, the people of Earth will have a Space Rangers Corps. The top recruits from the best military units from across the globe, joined together. Ready to protect the planet from any extraterrestrial threats. Ready to take our first ships into deep space to discover what lies beyond the solar system, and return. Representatives of Earth. Representatives of a United Earth."

"Turner, it may have stared out as a yawner, but you may have something," Booth said. "But we are going to need more production and stage show if we expect the UEC to fund the Space Rangers Project. Here's what you are going to do . . ."

Turner called the important scientists together for a symposium at UEC's campus in Toronto. He invited others; scientists, and well-known media types unaware of the different projects, to attend and act as unbiased critics. For two weeks they reviewed data, discussed risks and rewards, and decided, by an eighty-two percent majority of opinion, science could re-engineer a human to be stronger, faster, healthier, resistant to disease and capable of regenerating at a cellular level to the point of an extended lifespan of potentially thousands of years. The advent of a true meta-human was possible.

Mattson-Grimes' marketing staff made sure all UEC members were made aware of the symposium. Several attended lectures, or dropped in on group discussions. PR people assured the representatives were given active roles in discussions, and not just left sitting on the sidelines.

Booth used her position to generate buzz. At the conclusion of the two weeks of round-robin meetings, once they had consensus, her office announced the UEC had created a way of making it possible for humans to endure the stress of extended space travel.

The Board of Governors, the real power behind the UEC, decided they wanted a military presence to secure the role of a proposed Space Fleet branch of the military. The Space Ranger Project would create a company, 250 strong, to become the rock Space Fleet would build upon. People dedicated to their military roots, in the prime of physical fitness, with field experience and higher than average IQs would be recruited. They would need to be mentally strong with adventurous personalities. They would come from every corner of the globe.

At the UEC's request, scientists, medical doctors, psychologists, psychiatrists, and military experts developed a profile as the template for a Space Ranger. Once it was completed and approved, the UEC issued a request for volunteers.

Turner Mattson-Grime's public relations campaign launched. The Space Rangers' Project made the news, everywhere.

Just After Before the Beginning, But Still Before the Beginning -

Captain Daniel "Coop" Cooper lazed on the front porch of his assigned on-base living quarters in Tunis, Tunisia. Acting company leader for ninety-two soldiers of the North African Battalion of the Can-American Army Rangers. His butt in a rocker, and his feet on the porch railing. All things seemed good at the moment.

His company completed five search-and-destroy missions, and another three rescue-and-recover missions in the previous twelve weeks. Currently in the middle of a seventy-two hour break, Coop contemplated the back of his eyelids. His field tablet, setting on the porch next to his rocker, alerted him to an incoming message.

The UEC dispatch requested volunteers for an experimental project. They intended to create a company of Rangers for deployment in outer space. The experiment included the possibility of genetic enhancements, and carried a high degree of risk. The rewards included the opportunity to join the new Space Fleet branch, where Rangers would actively engage in security and exploration of both the solar system and nearby star systems. The dispatch did not list the specific risks. If interested, complete the attached application and return it within one week.

With nothing better to do, Coop spent the lazy afternoon filling out the application. On the Martian morning Fairchild discovered the alien space ship on Mars, Coop was five-years old. Like every kid everywhere, he dreamed about space travel, aliens, and adventure. A resurgence of twentieth and twenty-first century sci-fi serials and movies catered to his young imagination. Turning in the form was a crap shoot, but worth the tiny effort, so he completed every question and hit the reply button.

The UEC dispatched 50,184 requests for application. Data-mining, based on the final profile, selected potential applicants from personnel files of military, police, and affiliated para-military groups. 20,801 applications returned. These were forwarded to the psi-ops specialists. Applications included embedded questions to help determine the mental readiness of the applicants, as well as potential emotional reactions to the genetic altering process. It required two months to pare the list to 11,980.

Five-months, twelve-days after Coop hit REPLY, and half the world away, a nondescript female psy-ops staffer stood before Booth, ready with updates, and prepared to answer questions.

"You may begin anytime," the UEC rep told the staffer. She was engaged rubbing her left foot, left leg crossed, and her dark blue business skirt hiked up high enough to show panties, if the Governor wore panties.

"Yes, ma'am." The young woman focused on the portrait of Canada's first Prime Minister, John A. Macdonald, hanging behind the actual woman. "11,980 readiness surveys were sent to commanding officers. These officers were asked to rate the volunteers under their command in several categories. It required two weeks to get all of the reports back, and another two weeks to evaluate them. From this step, the number of potential candidates dropped to 6,000."

"Exactly 6,000?" Booth asked. "Round number, 6,000?"

The staffer's eyes lowered to meet Booth's eyes, dropped lower out of curiosity, and hurriedly returned to the portrait.

"Yes, ma'am. Exactly 6,000. Military experts, both current and retired, were tasked with the next step. They took the 6,000, and determined which ones excelled in most, if not all, of the following training programs, and how many had performed those programs while under battlefield conditions."

Her eyes dropped again, but this time to a data pad. She read off:

"SCUBA/Maritime Warfare
Arctic and Mountain Warfare
Sabotage and Demolitions
Parachute and HALO (High Altitude - Low Opening)
techniques
Long Range Reconnaissance
Counter-terrorism and CQB, meaning Close Quarter
Battle
Vehicle insertion
Sniping
Hand-to-Hand Combat
SERE, which stands for Survival, Escape, Resistance
and Evasion."

Her eyes rose, discovered the world leader had dropped her leg and was no longer flashing. Able to make eye contact, she continued her report.

"Following two months of," she read from her pad, "reading after-action reports, command reports, commendations, and recommendations for promotions and medals, plus all other reports collected by organizations on their personnel, two-thousand eighteen volunteers were selected to attend the Fleet Assessment Training in Nevada, USA."

Almost To The Beginning -

Five-months, twenty-days after sending in his application, Coop's field tablet alerted him to the message inviting him to begin Space Fleet Ranger training in Nevada in one month. His commanding officer and line of command copied the same alert. He received a four-week furlough to get his things, grab down time, and report to the designated airfield in Las Vegas, where he would be airlifted to the secure training facility.

Coop, dressed in comfortable but functional field clothing without rank or insignias, and his favorite desert boots, arrived at the appointed time (6:00am CMT), at the appointed place (Las Vegas Airfield). He, and two-thousand seventeen others, piled into unmarked, distinctly military, transport planes. At 6:15am they took off. At 6:45am they landed.

No one was allowed to grab their packs. Instead, groups of ten were placed on military transport hover-copters and flown into the Nevada badlands. It required twenty choppers ten trips each, plus a couple of extra, to take all of the volunteers into the desert and deposit them anywhere from fifty to sixty-miles from the staging area.

Coop's group reached sixty-miles out when their hover craft landed. The Gunny on the doorway railgun told them "Out."

When the final pair of boots hit the rocky ground, he yelled, "You have twenty-four hours to make it back to base. You don't make it back, or you don't make it back it under twenty-four, your gear will be on a transport taking you back where you came from. Or your body will be sent to next of kin."

No other instructions were forthcoming. No comments or questions allowed. Gunny slammed the door shut, and the chopper flew away. Coop noted the craft continued on the same heading flown to deliver them to the drop zone. The pilot was not going to provide a hint which direction the base was located.

"On me," shouted a twenty-something US Marine: complete with jarhead haircut, and wearing camo desert BDUs. "I am United States Marine Corps First Lieutenant Charles Hammond, and unless anyone objects, I will take command." No one commented, including Coop, who out-ranked the Marine, but wanted to see him in action. "We have sixty miles to cover over desert terrain. We need to average three-miles-per-hour to insure we arrive well within our allotted time."

He pointed east, where the sun was rising. "The chopper came in from that direction. I'll take lead. Single file. Let's motor people. I do not intend on returning to San Diego tomorrow."

Hammond took off in a fast jog, followed by eight others. Cooper stayed back, watching as they disappeared over a rocky hill. He began walking in the same general direction, but twenty-degrees north of the L.T.'s line.

He travelled a quarter-mile, when he heard footsteps running up from behind. Looking over his left shoulder he found a female in khaki cargo pants, jump boots, and a black t-shirt catching up to him. She wore a baseball cap, also black, pulled low over her eyes. Average height, and lean, she still made the t-shirt bounce as she ran. Once she caught up, she slowed to match his pace.

"¿Que pasa?" she asked.

"Nada," Coop replied. "Why'd you leave the looey?"

"Wasn't so much leaving him," she answered in English, with no discernible accent, "as it looked like you might be smarter. So, are you smarter, amigo?"

"More observant," Coop replied. "The chopper didn't fly a straight line. It was subtle, but it made a soft arch, slipping south to southwest, before flying the last couple of minutes west. Probably added twenty miles, and took us over some unremarkable hilly terrain so we wouldn't notice. Who are you?"

"Captain Elena Casalobos, Caballero Legionario Maderal Oleaga," she replied, raising a two-finger salute to her cap's brim.

"The Diecinueve," Cooper said. "Spain's 19th Special Operations group. You guys have a reputation older than Delta Force's. Originally the Spanish Legion, if my memory serves. And a Captain. Why did you let United States Marine Corps First Lieutenant Hammond take command of the group?"

"Wanted to see him in action. I figure not everyone is going to make the cut, so better to shut up, and watch the competition," she answered, adding a smile. "When I noticed you weren't behind me, I thought I'd see why."

"And you didn't bother to tell the person in front of you?"

"Nope. Figured if you were hurt, and couldn't walk, I could catch back up. If you were as smart as you are pretty, maybe you had a better plan. You know my name and rank, soldier, so how about you."

"Captain Daniel Cooper, Can-Am Rangers, recently North Africa Battalion," he answered with a two-fingered return salute. "And not too many people have ever called me pretty."

"So what's the plan, Daniel?" she asked, continuing to match his pace.

"Coop," he said. "Friends call me Coop, and the plan is to walk a little ways. I'm looking for a place to spend the hottest part of the day. We double time once it gets cooler."

They walked in comfortable silence for five hours. The sun, and the temperature rising as their shadows grew shorter. Coop eventually spotted what he was looking for, and veered them left, forty-yards off their course. He stopped before a hillside with an overhang, rocky sides, and a sandy base. He picked up a dried stick from a long dead tree, and started poking around the sand under the over-hang, near where the rocks came all the way to the ground. After a minute, he dropped to his knees, and began clearing away sand. He uncovered a rocky basin, with an inch-to-two of water.

"So do your other friends also call you Moses?" Casalobos asked.

"Desert trick. Rain water will follow the rocks down, and sometimes you have rock beneath the sand. If you're lucky it forms a catch. The shade from the overhang keeps it from evaporating for a few days. The scrubby bush around here is a little greener, so it made sense to look. And there are foot-prints in the sand from coyote, or desert fox. Often you need to search several locations, and sometimes you never find water. Finding it on the first try is a combination of luck, and it must have rained in the last day or two."

"Don't think much about luck. You've been looking for this exact spot. What do we do about the sand in the water?" she asked.

"Give it a couple of minutes to settle. You can scoop from the top," he explained. "We lay up in the shade, have some water, get some sleep, and in a few hours continue."

"Sounds like a plan," she said, gliding into a lotus position in the shade of the overhang. "Don't you feel bad about leaving the other seven with the Marine?"

"There's an old saying about elections . . . who's the bigger fool, the fool, or the fool who follows a fool?"

Coop dropped into a cross-legged sit, next to the Spaniard.

Nodding her understanding, and agreement, Elena closed her eyes, and soon lingered in a space between calm and sleep. Coop joined her.

Six hours later, with the desert sun casting long shadows stealing back to the East, the two drank more water before taking off, returning to the line Cooper followed earlier. This time at an easy jog. When dark arrived it would come with a three-quarter moon, and while footing would be hazardous, there would be enough light for them to pick up the pace. Coop led with Elena close behind.

According to Coop's chronometer, it was 18:39pm CMT when they departed the water hole. He set a five-mph pace. Faster than he would have taken troops on a desert mission, but he did not need to fear booby-traps, or snipers in the Nevada desert. He also wanted to see how Casalobos held up. Like she said, it was never too soon to evaluate the competition.

They picked up the faint lights of the base camp at 3:00am. At 3:32am they jogged onto the airfield, and were met by a medical team. They each had vitals measured and each provided a sample of blood. They were not the first to arrive, but they were back with three hours to spare.

A full-bird Can-Am Army Colonel approached, and both snapped to attention. "As you were," he said. "Where's the rest of your team?"

"We're our team," Casalobos said. "The other eight went a different direction."

"And you let them?"

"Wasn't part of the mission details," Coop responded. "We were told to get back within twenty-four hours, not get everyone back in twenty-four hours."

"Would you leave your people in the desert on a mission, Captain Cooper?"

The Colonel was not angry, just asking a question, while a medic handed him an old-fashion clipboard with paper sheets attached.

"Depends on the mission, sir," Coop replied.

"Captain Casalobos, same question."

"What he says," she said, and added, "sir."

"According to your med report, neither of you show signs of dehydration after spending a day in the desert."

Since the statement had not been phrased as a question, neither replied.

When no explanation was forthcoming, the Colonel told them, "Your bags are over by the hangar. Find 'em, go inside. An ensign will take you to your assigned bunks." The two Captains came to attention. "Dismissed," the Colonel said, walking away to question another soldier.

The hangar was not only a hangar. The Navy ensign, a tall female with a by-the-book approach to life, led them to an elevator. Perhaps de-elevator a more appropriate description. They dropped at least four stories. The Ensign led Casalobos to room 404, and Cooper, further down the hallway, to 414. Elena gave Coop a half-wave, half-salute, which he returned before entering his new home.

He made a quick inventory. Over-sized bunk with linens folded on top, and two pillows; a desk, and chair with computer station; a closet, dresser, and a private head with shower and sink. He had lived with less.

He tossed his bag at the foot of the bed, and placed his dirty, sweaty baseball cap on the dresser. He looked forward to a shower, but before getting any nearer the reward, a knock sounded at his door. Opening it, he found Captain Elena Casalobos, who smiled, came in without an invitation, and inspected his room.

"Same as mine," she told him. She dropped a small go bag on his bunk, and began taking her sweat-stained t-shirt off. "And a friend would help me scrub this sand off. It's gotten into some pretty tight spaces."

Naked she turned on the water, and when it was no longer cold, stepped into the stall. Coop joined her.

The Middle -

1,683 volunteers returned to the base camp in time, or close enough, to continue. United States Marine First Lieutenant Charles Hammond, and those with him, were not part of the cut. Over the next six weeks, the goal, for those in charge, was cut the number of volunteers to a final two-hundred fifty. These special operators would comprise Earth's first company of Space Rangers.

Week 1. Things Fall Down.

Flight insertion is the ability to start your parachute jump at a designated altitude, and end up within a targeted area. Originally, High Altitude and Low Opening, or Low Altitude and Low Opening training consisted of jumping from as high as 35,000 feet, with bail-out oxygen, free falling to a couple of hundred feet above target, opening your chute, and landing quickly, quietly, and whole. Or, in LALO, do the same thing from a couple of thousand feet up, with no O2, and less free fall.

Each volunteer performed one HALO, one LALO, and one of the two picked by the Jump Master based on his opinion of their weakest attempt.

Eighty-four candidates were injured, or failed to land within the target zone in any of their three attempts.

The remaining candidates hit the target in one, two, or all three jumps. Two modern variations were added. Jumpers exchanged paraglide chutes for free-flight wing-suits. The latest incarnation of the wing-suit allowed a jumper to leave from heights up to 15,000 feet, without oxygen, or higher with it. They could either deploy a small parachute for the final segment of the flight and the landing, or, if sufficiently skilled, or crazy, or both, could actually bring themselves onto target without deploying the safety drag-parachute.

Coop accomplished the second longest jump, nearly ten-minutes in the air, hitting the fifty-foot target without deploying the drag-chute. The black 'batwing'-suit flared at the last second, when he whipped his body out and up, landing upright.

Casalobos bettered his time by a full minute, and landed ten-feet closer to the center of the bull's eye.

One-hundred twelve volunteers either refused to use the wing-suits, missed the target three of three tries, or were injured landing and could not continue.

The reward for the 1,571 remaining were motorized hover-chutes, and unsupervised time on the desert.

Coop, having completed a few loops across the terrain, joined Casalobos in the shade of a transport. She had gone out earlier, thoroughly enjoyed the time in the air, and now enjoyed the respite in the shade.

She tossed him a cold water, which he opened and began drinking as he swiveled and sat cross-legged beside her.

"You have eyes for the skinny brunette," she said. Her black ball-cap covered her eyes in shadow, but it was obvious the direction of her gaze.

A tall, slender female with short brown hair leaned against a cargo box. She tracked the flight of a hover-chute with eyes so green the color obvious from fifty-feet away.

"I heard her talking with another guy," Coop said. "Something familiar about her voice. Couldn't place it, but I'm pretty sure I've heard it before."

"So why not introduce yourself?" the Spaniard asked. "Ask her if she knows you. Maybe it was dark. She might have whispered things."

"No, I would remember those eyes," Coop said. "If I don't remember soon, I'll ask."

"Just don't remember when you're on top of me. That would be rude."

Week 2. Things Look Up.

1,487 began Week Two by loading into unmarked troop transport planes, and flying to a private airfield outside of Longmont, Colorado. From the strip, everyone could see Long's Peak, rising 9,000 feet above the western edge of the Great Plains.

No one bothered to explain the eighty-four missing people. Could be illness, or discipline, or home-sickness. Some people just drop out. One thing for sure, it was not because of fraternization. Coop and Elena spent every free moment, including nights, together, and they were still present.

A Can-Am Army Ranger Master Sergeant, with the Mountain Unit Patch on his left shoulder, addressed the assembly.

"You will divide into teams of eight, with one team of seven. There are packs with climbing gear in the hangar to your left. Once you have teamed up, and have your gear, one person from each team will stick their hand in a hat, and select a direction. That will indicate which face of the mountain you will ascend. Another will select a number; either number one, or number two. Finally another team member will pull a one, two, or three." Master Sergeant waited, and was pleased when no comments were made.

"The first number, one or two, indicates whether you go today, or tomorrow. If today, you ride out. If tomorrow, you make camp here. Cots are in the hangar. The second number indicates whether your group ascends first, second, or third. There will be a half-hour lapse between teams. Each face offers multiple routes. You decide which one you team takes.

"Each route requires different options, and each option requires different degrees of expertise. Your team's combination of choices and proficiency will result in differing amounts of time to ascend, and then descend from the peak. We have average times for each face as completed by a squad of Mountain Unit Rangers. You have to complete your climb and descent within thirty-percent of the time set by the Rangers. Any team failing to meet their mark, everyone on the team will be sent home." He hesitated again. Again, no comments.

"We have transport to the base of Long's Peak, that big damn mountain over there [and he pointed]. At the top, it is 12,000 feet above sea level. There are fourteen different ascent routes available. Since it is late spring, you will not have to deal with too much snow or ice, but it is still wet, slick, and dangerous."

The Master Sergeant turned away from the mountain. "Back here in thirty, as teams. Dismissed."

Coop and Elena watched hundreds of others rush to the hangar to grab equipment. A young Japanese man joined them.

"I am Hiroshi Kimura. I would like to be on team with you," and he actually bowed. Elena bowed back, but Coop offered his hand, which was taken.

"I'm Coop and this is Elie," he said.

"Elie?" Casalobos queried, hearing the shortened version of her name for the first time.

"Nickname," Coop replied. "Easier, quicker, and on a climb we need to communicate quickly. Okay?"

She shrugged, and looked back to Kimura, who had watched the exchange closely, deciding he liked the two gai-jin. "Buenos Dias, I am Elie."

"Please call me Hiro. It will be quicker," he replied.

Another four volunteers walked up, asked about joining, and all were accepted.

One of them, a young woman with short blonde hair, asked, "Shouldn't we get equipment?"

"The kits will all be the same, so first or last doesn't matter," Coop told her. "Right now, not getting trampled is more important."

When half of the others returned to the air strip, and were trying to establish teams, Coop suggested they retrieve their kits.

Elie drew the first piece of paper from a bucket, not a hat. The draw would dictate from which direction they would attack the mountain. "East," she said.

Hiro picked from the next bucket, and called, "One."

The young, blonde female, a US Naval Rescue Swimmer named Samantha, selected from the third bucket, and called, "Three."

Ground transports were marked according to locations, so the team boarded one marked 'EAST'. Twenty-eight miles later, they stepped off at the eastern foot of Long's Peak.

The East Face proved to be the steepest possible ascent to the peak. A one-thousand foot wall dominated the early ascent, and included routes named the Diamond, and the Lower East Face. All climbs here appeared technical, from 5.10 to 5.13. One face looked like an upside-down Diamond, thus the name.

From Coop's position, facing the mountainside, it seemed possible to climb to the left of the Diamond's face proper, using free-style only. There were numerous cracks, ledges for finger, and toe holds. The routes on the right side of the Diamond would require aids, like pitons and ropes. Climbers would require spending recovery time on the left wall, and the rocks there looked wet.

"Left or right?" Elie asked.

"While the left side would be quicker, only a qualified climber should attempt it," Coop remarked. Cooper was qualified, and knew Elie could handle it, but was unsure of the other five. "We're climbing against time, but speed will be determined by the weakest climber. Army Rangers would have taken the left side, and would have set times hard to beat by even experienced climbers."

Cooper silently calculated variables, considering the effects of altitude and the alpine conditions, in addition to the difficulty. He made an educated guess at how long it would take him to free climb Diamond, and added thirty percent.

While he was considered a desert specialist, he did completed the mountain course for Rangers. In fact, his father had been the Commander in charge of the Mountain Training program in Dahlonega, Georgia, since Coop was five. Appalachian mountains were older, and smaller, but some of the climbs every bit as difficult as ones in the Rockies.

Joining Cooper would be Elena, a Spaniard, Hiro, the Japanese, an Israeli female named Ziva, a German male, Michael, and two Americans, Ken, and Samantha. He did not care where they were from, what they believed, or what sex they were. His only concern was their climbing experience. He discovered he, Elie, and Michael were military certified climbers, with experience. The others, not so much, though Hiro promised he was an excellent, if uncertified, climber.

Cooper checked the bags. They included sleeping nets. He had four team members with limited to zero mountain experience, so the decision was easy.

"We take the right side. Either Elie, Mike, or I will lead. We have compression pitons, so we will clamp them into cracks or crevices, and feed ropes back. There are climb aiders in the packs. If you have any trouble with hand-over-hand, just attach the aider, and use it like a ladder. The first half of the climb will be tough, but if everyone stays hooked in, there shouldn't be anything so technical we all can't make it."

He turned to face the mountain, and pointed toward the top.

"We'll take a rest about three-quarters up. There's a small ridge there. If it's wide enough, maybe we just sit, and let our lungs catch up. If it isn't, we set the sleep nets, and rest for a couple of hours. The last section is the steepest. It will take the most strength, and probably as much time as the first three-quarters."

"If we aren't tired, we shouldn't stop," the American, Ken, said. "We're against the clock."

"If we get there, and your lungs, legs, and arms aren't on fire from the work and the altitude, then you go right ahead," the German responded. "In the mean time, we have an hour to wait, so we might as well rest."

Coop and Elie grabbed packs, and did a thorough inventory of all supplies. Both wore heavyweight BDU's, so they stashed smaller gear and nutrition bars in pockets. Backpacks received water, along with extra pitons, clamps, carabiners, and a wet-dry towel. As they uncoiled the 125-foot dry rope each had, the others took the clue, and began prepping for the climb.

An hour passed before the first group started up the right side. The seven watched their progress, and the line they decided to ascend. Thirty minutes later, an all-male team started up the left side. They carried two ropes, and minimal gear. They were free-climbing, relying on speed, and strength to get them up and over.

"They have the time bug," Cooper said. "They're hooked on making the best time possible, instead of making a time good enough. Wish 'em luck."

At 10:56am their group was called.

"It's going to take eight to ten hours, so the last bit will be in dusk to dark. Keep that in mind. Conserve energy when, and where you can. Lead climber sets the pace. Hiro, please handle the six." Seeing his lack of comprehension, he explained, "You are last man up."

Three hours on course, they caught the first group up. The initial team on the face climbed in a line, taking an ascent to the right of the route Coop selected. They moved at a deliberate, cautious pace. Altitude, and early speed had caught up with at least two of the team. Now the entire group had to make the climb one step at a time. The free climbers to the left were visible, and two-hundred feet higher, making good time.

The flash-boom caught everyone by surprise.

Colorado is famous for apocalyptic lightning storms, especially those to roll in during the afternoons. The people in charge were either taken by surprise by the storm's arrival, or they simply did not care about the weather.

Dark clouds from the West rolled over the top of the mountain. The peak had shielded the incoming storm from sight, until the first crack of lightning. The next bolt hit a ridge above them, and the resulting boom made teeth rattle. This was going to be a ground event; not sky-to-sky.

Cooper quickly pulled everyone up to his position. When Hiro arrived, the rain arrived with him. The wet rocks now ran with rain water, and the dark mountainside lit by strobes of deadly lightning.

Coop shouted to be heard. "You can't outrun, or out climb a storm. Physics win every time. There is a rock fall about twenty-feet up, and to our right. It looks to be about thirty-five feet tall. If we can get within a cone of ten feet, lightning will be more likely to strike it than us.

"When the lightning hits, it will send a current through the ground. Try to keep your weight on your shoes. The rubberized soles will help insulate you. Do not grab cracks unless you absolutely have to. Leave the ropes. Wet ropes act like conductors. Drop your bags, and make sure all metal is in the bags. Pitons, carabineers, anything metal. Leave it in your bag, and tie it to the rope. Once we get over there, separate. Do not bunch together. Find a flat spot, and crouch down. Avoid anyplace where water is pooling. Get to it people."

Each member removed any metal equipment, and stored it in their bags. They velcroed the bags to the rope. Slowly, because of the slippery rocks and the darkness, all seven made it to within fifteen feet of the outcropping. Coop made sure no one stopped in the gaps between the loose boulders where sparks could find them. He also checked to see there was space enough between them. If one person did get hit, they would not take anyone with them.

The seven remained crouched, with heads down, hoods up, and arms locked around knees for the forty minutes it took the storm to blow over. Ken started to get up, and Coop yelled at him.

"Wait another few minutes. The storm is over, but lightning can strike from as far away as five miles. Give it another twenty before we regroup."

Twenty minutes later Coop reformed his group. He checked on the climbers who had been on their right, and got a thumb's up when he yelled to them.

The free climbers on the left had not been as lucky. Two had slipped, sliding down over one-hundred feet. They hung one above the other, fingers desperately jammed into cracks. From his advantage, Coop could not see any finger or foot holds which would allow them to move up, down, left, or right. They were lucky to have stopped at all on the sleek surface of the face.

The other six were plastered against the wall, unable to help the two below.

Coop and Elie grabbed bags, and recovered ropes. They free-climbed the next one hundred feet. Mike and Hiro remained behind to tie-off with the two Americans and the Israeli. They followed at a safer pace.

Coop and Elie stopped parallel to the stranded climbers. After assessing the conditions from this angle, Coop scaled another twenty feet, and set a double piton into a crevasse. He swung over to the lower climber, grabbed him around the chest, and swung back, where Elie could grab both of them. He went up again so he would have the proper angle, and repeated the process with the second climber. By the time they had both men off the shear face, Mike arrived. They handed the two off. The two shaken climbers could join the others on rope-line, once the others arrived.

Coop, with Elie on his heels, climbed another hundred-feet to find a place to extract the remaining six free-climbers. The two began the exhausting repetition of climb, swing, grab, and recover six more times. Elie would have taken

more of the load, but it required Coop's strength to physically grab each stranded man, and carry him on the swing to
where she waited.

The following group arrived in time to assist Elie, grab-
bing Coop and his human baggage, the final two trips.
Everyone helped get the six hooked onto the rope line. All
eight turned out to be amateur rock climbers. They had decided to team up because of their shared experience. None
had ever faced a challenge like the Diamond delivered. High
altitude sapped their energy, and the storm had taken the
fight out of them.

When they recovered, their added strength meant the
two teams, working together, could make the final ascent
without difficulty. It would just take time for them to rally.
They could continue at a slow pace, allowing their lungs to
adapt.

Coop was exhausted as well. He needed to rest, and not
while on the move. Elie refused to leave him, so the two un-
elected leaders directed the others ahead. Hiro was the last
to depart.

"I should stay," he said. "It is not fair the two of you have
done so much of the work, and, yet, will not make the time. I
do not know if even we will make it."

"Go," Coop told him. "You still have to descend. We'll
catch you somewhere along the way."

They watched Hiro climb. He was actually a strong
climber. They observed his efforts from their backs, lying on
a tiny ridge together. They ate protein bars, drank water, and
Elie said, "You know, we'll never catch them."

"Sleep is a weapon," he said cryptically. "I'll wake you in
ninety minutes."

Ninety-one minutes later, he said, "The most difficult part of the Diamond's face are the overhangs down below. Once you get past them, it's a fairly simple slope."

"Are you suggesting we swing over to the other side, and free climb to the top?"

"Yep."

"Cool," she replied.

Soon both switched from the right side, to the left side of the mountain's eastern face. Coop released the rope, and re-coiled it. He had his backpack on, the rope around a shoulder. Elie did the same. They pulled chalk-bags from their packs, and snapped them onto their belts.

Two hours later, they caught the hybrid team to cheers, and a couple of friendly cat-calls. An hour more, and they stood at the crest. They waited, and rested two hours for the others to complete the more technical, but less physically taxing route.

Elie and Coop received bear hugs by their original team, and again by the second team. Elie getting longer hugs by the second team's members.

"It's going to be a bitch getting back down," Mike said. "We're all tired, and it's getting darker. Even the Army Rangers had to stop and rest before returning, don't you think?"

"Probably," Coop agreed, "but we aren't going down that way."

"We have to, or get disqualified," a free-climber team member commented, having overheard the conversation.

"Nope," Coop answered. "The Master Sergeant said specifically, we had to ascend the route selected. He didn't say a damn thing about the descent. On the drive over, I no-ticed the northern face. Some civilian climbers were repelling down, and they were dropping straight, and fast. I say we hike over there, and do the same."

"Anyone with a better idea," Elie asked out loud, and with no response, or argument, the fifteen combined climbers followed a well-marked trail to the crest of Long's north face.

"Damn," the German said. "They have permanent pitons, and cable holds installed. Looks like they are set in all the way down. Look, a group is about half-way down."

They descended the northern route, taking half the time it would have taken to traverse the eastern face. The two teams joined three groups of eight at the bottom for the crowded ride back to the base. Six climbers rode on top of the transport, which had been sent to collect twenty-four candidates, but returned with thirty-nine back.

Coop had been right. No one cared how they got down. Plus, he , Elie, and their team were given special recognition by the Master Sergeant for the rescue and recovery of the free-climbers.

On the third day after arriving, they boarded unmarked planes for the return trip to Nevada. Four people had been killed by lightning, another three killed during the climbs, and twenty-three badly injured. 656 climbers on 82 teams did not return within the thirty-percent time limit.

801 volunteers remained after just the first two weeks of trials.

Week 3. Things Go Boom.

Week three consisted of two days of training, followed by performance in sabotage, and demolition techniques. Since no one blew themselves up, while managing to successfully blow up a bunch of old junk, everyone passed. Nine people quit on their own.

During the week, Coop and Hiro discovered a mutual love of martial arts, and weapons. They agreed to meet in one of the training studios to practice. Practices soon became sparring matches.

Week 4. Things Get Close.

Close Quarter Battle (CQB) is either small teams fighting in tight locations, like trying to take an enemy hiding within a city, or the rescue of hostages from a space controlled by bad guys. It is small arms, and hand-to-hand combat, usually involving knives. Since every volunteer in the program was proficient at personal battle techniques, the Space Ranger Project was more interested in how they operated within a team, and under stress.

Command divided those left into two groups of 396. By blind draw, these two groups again sub-divided into ninety-nine four-person teams.

An officer presented a scenario to a team from Group A, and put them on the clock while they decided on a strategy. Next, they implemented their plan, to either take out a group of enemy combatants, or rescue a hostage. A team from Group B was given the exact same scenario.

Seasoned Can-Am Rangers played the roles of enemy combatants. Hostages were dummies. Straw dummies, not stupid for getting caught by the bad guys. A panel of experienced officers and NCOs graded each team on planning, execution, and results.

The panel compared the team results, and issued grades. One team would advance, and the other team was history.

On day five, Coop answered a knock at his door. Elie walked by, and dropped onto his bunk.

"My team made it though," she told him. "I lucked out. Hiro was on my side. The guy is a shadow. Someone said he isn't even military. We had to go into a room blind, and rescue a hostage. He went in first, and by the time we followed, all we had to do was untie the dummy."

"Doesn't exactly fit the narrative of 'team' work," Coop observed.

"Does if you have a fucking ninja on your team," she replied.

"My team had a close-quarter firefight. We were outnumbered, and outgunned, but we had the high ground, and better shooters. There was a Russian Special Ops guy named Gregory on my team. The guy could shoot a gnat off a golf ball in flight. If anyone showed skin, he took it off. I understand we're down to three-ninety-six."

"I understand we have a couple of days off," Elie said. "Unless you object, I intend on spending them right here."

"No objections."

Week 5. Things Go Bang.

The fifth week involved pure skill. Everyone required to perform with short, and long-range weapons, both laser and projectile.

It was simple. Six shots at a target. Targets placed at different distances. Pistol, laser pistol, rifle, laser rifle, and finally, a sniper's weapon, not of your own choice. Points for closest to center.

Anton Gregory hit a center from over 2,000 yards, using a sniper's rifle he had never handled before.

"You let him beat you."

Coop turned to the ebony-skinned woman. "I've seen you with a rifle. Why did you miss?"

"Hell-o, Sindy. I didn't miss. I just didn't hit center," he replied.

"On purpose," she countered. "You're always so damn honest, Coop. Easier to remember the truth than a lie. Always let the person know where they stand. Have you decided lying is okay now?"

"I also taught you to keep some of your cards hidden," he replied. "Being number one on the range or number one-hundred means the same when the top one-hundred receive the same reward."

The dark beauty gave him a steel-eyed gaze with brown eyes wrinkled at the edges from the harsh African sun.

"Win the game, not the practice," she said. "I remember the things you taught me. Took them back to Ethiopia and made Captain in the Agazi Commandoes."

"Hey, Coop. Who's your friend?" Elie asked, joining them at the watchers' station set at the rear of the rifle-laser range.

The Ethiopian commando turned to the Spanish commando and offered her a hand, which Elie took.

"I'm practice," she said. Letting Eli's hand go, she turned and walked away.

At the end of the week, twenty percent were cut, leaving 316 volunteers, and one more week of trials.

Week 6. Things Get Lighter.

The underground facility housing the Space Ranger Project was huge. Besides the space to bed over 3,000 people, there were hangars, storage, kitchens, mess halls, training facilities, shooting ranges, fitness centers, and recreation halls. The complex enclosed separate sections for science, military operations, and a complete medical wing. There was also a gymnasium-sized arena where gravity could be manipulated. It could be made gravity free, or less-than-normal, or more intense.

Day 1 involved working at fifty-percent gravity. Volunteers had to move boxes, run and leap around obstacles, and climb walls. All in all, it was a fun day for everyone.

Day 2 provided more fun when the gym was made gravity free. Now they needed to traverse the gym, using, or avoiding obstacles floating in the air above the floor. More than a few made mistakes in propulsion, finding themselves banging off the roof, or slamming painfully into walls. One guy pushed so hard off the ceiling, angry over having hit it a second time, he landed on the floor, cracking his head. Three-fifteen remaining.

Day 3 was not so much fun. Day 3 was scary.

The science team introduced multi-directional mini-thrusters volunteers would wear on their belts. The little motors produced puffs of air, which would not do much in a gravitational field, but if you were weightless, they could get you moving, and keep you moving. Simple, too. Just twist the nozzle in the opposite direction you wanted to go, and push the button.

Small groups practiced together, leading to a lot of bumps and bruises. People had to look where they were going; look out someone, or someones were not about to careen into them; physically adjust the thruster, and push the thruster's button on, or off.

Days 4 and 5 were the cut-down days. Potential Space Rangers were provided helmet and vests with target sensors. Each person issued a laser-tag pistol. In five-against-five, in a gravity-free gym, with obstacles as cover, they had to get from one wall to the opposite wall, without getting lit up.

The extra five were paired against five individuals who had been tagged, but the training staff felt salvageable.

To make it more fair for individuals, teams were broken up after each fight, and people reassigned into new teams. This was repeated several times over the two days.

By close of the fifth day, ninety-five recruits had been tagged multiple times, and asked to leave. Two-hundred twenty of the original 20,801 applicants remained. They were given the weekend off. They could not leave the secure, and secret base, but they were not expected to perform any more tasks. Just relax, and show up by nine-hundred hours on Monday for a final briefing.

Coop and Elie spent a considerable amount of the extra time in his cabin, in bed, celebrating. They woke at 5:00am on Monday. Elie left for her cabin to get ready. They would meet for breakfast at six, and go together to the final brief.

Week 7. Things Get Real.

The two-twenty assembled in the gymnasium. They sat on bleachers facing a podium, and a number of chairs placed behind the dais. Coop noted the Russian sniper, Gregory, and Hiro also made the final cut. He knew most of the others by face, if not by name. Some he had become quite friendly with. Elie and he were an open secret, and since no one in charge told them to stop sleeping together, they had not.

The slender brunette turned out to be Rachelle Paré of the Can-Am Navy. She was a pilot, and had saved his ass in Algeria, along with a company of Rangers. Her call sign had been *Orphan,* and he had been *Shooter One* on the radio. That was why her voice, and not her face, was familiar. He still had not approached her, even to thank her belatedly.

Senait Kebede, *Sindy*, also made the cut. She joined his rifle team in Tunisia before the Raid at Ajej where he had received a field commission to Second Lieutenant. She transferred in from the Ethiopian Army for advanced Ranger training and field experience.

They could not seem to stop themselves from getting into bed, which went against a lot of Army regs and his own personal rules regarding the people he commanded. He explained it to her when he said no more. She requested a transfer out, and he okayed the request.

Even if she still hated him, he felt a great deal of pride seeing she made the final cut.

The half-dozen chairs in front filled with a mix of brass and civilians.

A Navy admiral Coop did not recognize, took the podium at exactly nine-hundred.

"Ladies and gentlemen, I am Admiral Jonas Myerson. First, and foremost, let me congratulate all of you for successfully completing the tasks placed before you these past six weeks. We, all of us here [indicating those seated], have watched with great interest to see who would be joining us today.

"This is the point in time when you must make the final decision. A decision that will shape your destiny. Whether you move forward with the Space Rangers, or elect to step aside. It is totally your decision. To help you make your decision before the final, and most critical phase of the project, Dr. Conrad Potterdamn, the genetic engineer in charge of the project, will explain what is about to happen. Dr. Potterdamn."

The Admiral occupied an empty chair, as a thin, short man with thin, balding hair, and light grey eyes replaced him behind the podium. He adjusted the microphone height before speaking. He pulled note cards from a suit pocket, place them on the stand, and looked over the people seated on the bleachers. The scientist appeared comfortable speaking before a large group.

"I also give my congratulations. The on-going human gnome project isolated a sequence of gene pairs termed the 'Methuselah Sequence'. Four base pairs of genes within 25,000 total genes. This structure responsible for the creation of modern humans. There was a time, hundreds of thousands of years in the past, when a person's lifespan could be measured in centuries, not decades. People lived productively for hundreds of years. An environmental shift, most likely a movement of the Earth's axis, caused a great flood. A flood so massive, it nearly wiped mankind off the face of the planet. Among the many losses wrought by the catastrophe was human longevity. But buried within our collective RNA, remains the sequence. Our bodies still own the genetic codes which once allowed us to exist, and our minds thrive, over much longer periods of time than modern man experiences."

Potterdamn must have spent time lecturing to halls of eager wannabe scientists. He had the presentation down, and held everyone's attention.

"My team of genetic engineers, working with world renown biochemists, have developed artificial enhancement cocktails. Bio-chemical combinations, which increased the strength, speed, bone density, and self-healing attributes of test animals by nearly six-fold the average. The animals did not reject the cocktails, nor the physical improvements, because the ingredients were variations of organic material already found within their bodies.

"Years of labor spent discovering a cure for the Eastern Pandemic, also resulted in research that produced a special serum. A serum able to provide immunity against bacterial, and viral infections. This miracle will soon be available to the general public, and many of today's illnesses will simply disappear.

"The final building block needed to make the Space Ranger Project actionable came from Mars." He hesitated, the dramatic pause used to bring everyone's focus to his next words.

"The information discovered by Elliott Fairchild, and decoded by Nathan and Mara Trent, offered much more than how to achieve interstellar flight. One data set detailed research into re-engineering humanoids. That research, stored for eons on Mars, paralleled the same research being done currently on Earth. And it provided the final component for success."

He took another dramatic pause. It was not necessary. Everyone, those in the bleachers, guests seated behind the podium, and personnel scattered around the room, were now fully engaged.

"Ancient aliens created an organic gel to cocoon the body, and when activated by a specific combination of lasers, and electrical impulses, the gel insulate allowed the body inside to absorb the elements necessary to re-engineer itself from functioning being, to near super-being."

It was time for the Doctor to cut to the chase. He had the audience, and needed to close the deal.

"We have created a method of making it possible for humans to endure the stress, and extended time required for space travel."

There. That was the cheese.

"You must now decide if you will be the first to take the next step. If you decide to become a Space Ranger, you will enter a tank filled with the Martian gel. For twenty-four hours you will be immersed in a mixture of organic and in-organic materials, including the minerals, hormones, and chemicals blended to remake your bones hard as steel, your muscles incredibly dense, and your nerve responses unbe-lievably quick.

"At the same time, we will reactivate your Methuselah sequenced genes. When you emerge, you will face the possi-bility of near immortality. While you will not be the first humans enhanced by science, but you will be the most sig-nificantly altered. You will be re-designed to flourish in the unfriendly reaches of outer space."

Finished, Dr. Potterdamn returned to his seat. The Admi-ral retook the podium.

"All experiments, to date, have been successful. But you will be the first humans to undergo this transformation. By completing the exams, the tests, and the trials over the last six weeks, you now represent the best, the brightest, and the most physically and psychologically prepared military unit on the planet. We have no doubt of the success of the project, but you have to make a personal decision. Do you want the change that will recreate you? If you have ques-tions, please ask them now."

There were a series of questions from the serious, like *would this effect memory or emotional status* (like steroids), to flippant (maybe), like *would it make you impo-tent, or sexually enhanced.*

Then a SEAL named Amber asked the big question: "If we do this, are we officially Space Rangers?"

The Admiral answered, "Yes, unqualified. You will be the Rangers of Company A, Space Fleet, and that will never be taken from you. We expect within the next couple of years, the two-hundred and twenty people here today will be in charge of the training, and deployment of all the Rangers who follow."

He nodded at two soldiers standing at the wall facing the bleachers. They pulled on chords to unfurl a large, square banner.

The Earth on a black square, with a comet's tail bisecting the planet, and the comet's fiery head on a trajectory for the banner's right-upper corner, was revealed. The words, UE SPACE FLEET, in large block letters beneath the insignia.

"This patch will ride your right shoulder." He nodded again, and a second banner opened, revealing a huge red SFA on a six-pointed silver star. "Space Fleet Company A," he said loudly. "This will ride your left shoulder."

He allowed the spontaneous applause to die down, but it still echoed in the gym when he said, "If you wish to move forward, please exit the gym by the doors on your left. If you do not wish to complete the project, please exit the doors to your right. There is no shame, and there will be no blame for anyone who goes to the right," he assured everyone, though every soldier and sailor in the world knew better.

A captain, among the seated guests, stood, and yelled, "Ten Hut!"

All two-twenty stood to attention.

"Dismissed!"

All two-twenty exited left.

Almost The End Of The Middle -

They had the remainder of the day, and the coming night to themselves. They were not allowed to make contact with family, or friends outside of the complex. They had been off the grid since arriving in Nevada. Having made the final decision, there was no reason to discuss it with anyone, anyhow. No alcohol, tobacco, or medications were allowed.

Most took the downtime alone, watching videos, playing games, or just taking things easy. Coop and Hiro enjoyed a light sparring session. Coop using a bo (fighting stick), and Hiro, a Kendo sword made of battan. Hiro won, barely. Anton and Elie held a shoot-off. Old style projectile pistols at fifty-yards. Anton won, barely. The four ate dinner with another twelve volunteers at a long table in the mess. When people began breaking off, and heading back to their cabins, Coop and Elie left for his.

The next morning, recruits awoke to find instructions and directions slipped under their doors. Dress in sweats only. No undergarments, no socks. No breakfast. At eight-hundred hours report to elevators, and proceed to sub-basement Seven, where they would be met.

At sub-basement Level Seven, each volunteer was escorted to a private room, where they undressed, and received a mini-physical. A small amount of blood given, a mouth swab, and final physical measurements taken. Information to be used as baselines for following the change.

Adjoining each room, a slightly larger studio had been prepared with an enclosed translucent vat. The containment tank glowed with a yellow-green gel. A small laser array rested on a mobile platform above the vat. Wires ran to and from the tank, and attached at a staffed monitoring console. Because of properties within the gel, wireless signals did not work. Finding enough wiring for two-hundred twenty tanks proved nearly as daunting a task as any the potential Rangers faced getting to the tanks.

Coop, standing naked, was introduced to his monitor, Dr. Selena Bright. Dr. Bright, a fifty-something woman with pale skin, and white hair, gave him a reassuring smile. "I will be hooking up the electrodes, and will monitor your progress. At any sign of discomfort, or should any problem arise, I will be here to abort the process, and revive you. If you could stand there for a few more minutes, the assistant [who had escorted him from the elevator, and remained near ever since], will attach adhesive patches to your skin. Finally, I will attach the monitor leads, and check to make sure everything is reading properly."

All went well, and Dr. Bright asked him to step on the offered step-stool, and continue into the gel. He was not sure what to expect, but the gel was body temperature, had no odor, and was not sticky. It felt like a warm bath of milk. Bright attached four IV tubes to his wrists and forearms. He settled in, resting his head on a padded neck pillow.

In other studios, the procedure replicated two-hundred nineteen times.

"Once you are comfortable, we will begin a sedative drip, which will slowly put you to sleep. When you are under, we will insert a breathing tube, pinch your nose closed, cover your eyes, and make sure the corners of your mouth are also taped closed."

Bright's bedside manner was top notch. She calmly explained each step of the process, a formula used to keep patients calm, relaxed, and agreeable.

"We will remove the neck pillow, and your head will be lowered into the gel. You will be in the vat for twenty-four hours. You will not experience any discomfort. Perhaps you will dream," she conjectured.

"I, or another doctor, will be here every minute to monitor your vital signs, and your reaction to each step along the way. Do you understand?"

"Yes."

"Are you ready?"

"Yes."

Within five minutes, Coop slept. Bright and the assistant went to work, and soon his head disappeared into the gel.

The Middle End -

Coop was having trouble waking. Lights flashed in his blurry vision; his eyes stinging. An alarm rang outside, and echoed inside his head. Maybe it was only inside his head. No, it was an alarm. His throat ached horribly, and his mouth was parched.

He was becoming more aware. Fighting to clear his mind. He was not in the vat. He was on a floor. Why was he on the floor? Someone shook him, yelling something. His ears were filled with goop. Did they know his ears had gel in them?

The alarm was causing a headache. His chest hurt. His body hurt. He coughed, and fluid flew from his mouth. How could fluid come out of a dry mouth?

The gel finally leaked from his ears, and he heard the man shaking him ask, "What did you say? Cooper, what did you say?"

Coop realized his sore throat made it difficult for him to talk, but repeated, "Turn the fucking alarm off. It's killing me."

"He's alive," the guy shouted, a poor imitation of Gene Wilder. "Get him cleaned off, and into a bed. Maintain monitors, and do not let him slip away. Keep him awake, and keep him breathing."

The guy was gone, and two others took his place. They lifted him onto a gurney, and rushed him down a hallway. Lights flashing, alarms ringing, and people were everywhere. They were shouting, and crying. Then he was in a private room. Someone used sponges to wash the yellow and green gel off, careful not to remove any of the monitor leads, or patches. He was lifted and placed gently onto a bed.

A woman . . . nurse? doctor? orderly? leaned over him, and said, "Sorry. The breather tube was yanked out, and your throat is raw. I can barely hear you."

"Elie?" he repeated. "Casalobos," he clarified. "How?"

"I'll find out as soon as I can," she assured him. "You rest. Try to relax. All that matters right now is you're alive."

Coop's senses were returning. He realized something went wrong with the process. Whether it went bad for just him, some, or all, he had no clue. The alarms, and people hurrying about were not good signs. He needed to know about Elie, but he could not get up. His body would not respond. His right hand did lift, and he grabbed the safety rail on the side of the hospital bed. When he squeezed, the metal bent, squealed a low protest, and broke.

"Captain Cooper," it was the woman again, looking down at him. "Captain Casalobos is alive. She's still unconscious, but they have vital signs, and she appears to be fine, just out. Please, Captain, you have to relax. Your heart rate, and your blood pressure are dangerously high. I do not want to give you anything to calm you. Do you understand?"

Coop nodded. He forced his mind to relax, and his body to uncoil. He went to the quiet spot he created as a sniper, when on long surveillance. He could feel his heart slow, and the drums in his ears subsided.

"Good job, Captain," the woman said. "Stay calm. When I know everything, hell, when I know anything, I will let you know." And she was gone again.

The End Of The End Of The Middle -

"We don't know why?" Dr. Potterdamn admitted. He, the Admiral, and a half-dozen doctors, engineers, and scientists sat in a large conference room, with the twelve Space Ranger Project survivors.

Coop sat next to Elie, afraid to lose touch with her. Gregory, and Hiro had made it. Several people he knew on a first name basis were not with them.

The French-Canadian flyer, Paré, was present. He caught glimpses of her since the project began, but never made the time to introduce himself.

Sindy was with them. She sat staring at her hands, clasped in her lap. Her strong sense of presence diminished, but she lived and would recover her confidence.

Potterdamn continued, "At twenty-hours into the transformation, the gel solution turned an orange-red. It had never changed colors before. At twenty-two hours people started dying. Hearts simply stopped beating. Everyone was pulled out. Anyone without a heartbeat was administered advanced CPR, shock paddles, adrenal-shots and anything else our cardiology staff could conceive might help. You twelve either never stopped breathing, or started again after receiving electrical stimulation. No one else did. We don't know why. We don't know why you survived, or why they didn't."

Dr. Tuttle, a micro-biologist added, "If you look around, you can see the problem. There isn't anything the twelve of you have in common, either on a physical level, or on a micro-level. Mix of male and female. White, black, oriental, and mixed race. Tall and short. You're all of a similar age. A shared trait, but one derived from the pre-selection criteria.

"The two hundred-eight who died were of the same age. Physically superior. High intelligence. Emotionally well-balanced. Copies of you. Nothing to provide a marker to lead us to an answer."

Admiral Myerson took over. "You will be kept here for another two weeks, minimum. We will monitor you, examine you, and, most importantly, make sure there isn't anything present to further endanger you. I would appreciate it if you would all return to your assigned cabins. Doctors will be coming by to speak with you individually, and set up a schedule of examinations. Your questions, and I know you have many, will be answered on a one-to-one basis. For now, you are dismissed."

Coop, Elie, and the others filed out of the conference room, as did everyone else except the genetic engineer, Potterdamn, and Admiral Myerson.

"The Space Ranger Project is dead," Myerson said to Potterdamn. "Without knowing why some lived, and why some died, we cannot chance another failure like this."

"Not a failure," Potterdamn argued. "We have twelve genetically enhanced humans. The first true meta-humans. They are extraordinary."

"You have two-hundred and eight of the finest men and women our planet ever produced lying in body bags in the basement," the Admiral countered. "We have no clue as to why. If you did it again, maybe they would all die, or maybe only half. It's a crap-shoot. We're closing it down, all of it."

"We should be allowed to continue experimenting," Potterdamn replied. "We're on the edge of being able to make humans immortal."

"That is a major part of the potential problem, Doctor. You are going to have every rich, or powerful person on Earth demanding access to the project, just so they can live forever. Most will be so desperate, the chance it might kill them will be worth the risk. Qnly it's not. The wrong person gets in, and gets killed, and we have global wars again. It was worth it to staff Space Fleet, and worth it when we thought it was safe. You will not play God again, Doctor."

"But all of the research?" the geneticist almost begged.

"The research will be archived for someone in the future to access. Maybe when we explore space, we will find a race who can answer the questions. The science teams will be disbanded, and sent as far apart as possible. The equipment destroyed. Anyone trying to take notes off of the base will be locked away for a long time. Anyone who brakes their oath of secrecy will be dealt with harshly. I repeat . . . Space Ranger Project is no more."

The End of the Beginning and The Middle &

The Beginning of Something New -

"We have to leak the story," Mattson-Grimes said. "We have to let the world know about the Space Rangers who survived."

"The military placed a large, red CLASSIFIED stamp on the project, Turner. I believe they shoot people they cannot court martial."

Governor Booth's hand rested on the final report regarding the project, which rested on her desk. Only the most sensitive files were still maintained on paper. Paper could not be hacked. Chemically treated paper would burn to ashes in seconds. Paper could be milled so it could not be copied, or digitally remastered.

"Besides, why would we want to announce such a horrid blunder to the world?"

"Madam Governor, the Space Rangers are meta-humans." The marketing and PR guru used the term in a hushed, reverent tone. "They can perform impossible feats, and they may be immortal. The project was a success. Limited, but a success. By letting people know some survived, it will give them hope."

"Hope?" Booth needed some hope herself. The project had cost a fortune, with no return on the investment. "Hope for what?"

"Hope we will discover why these twelve lived, so maybe one day we can dispense super powers to everyone. Hope these twelve will make a difference in the world. Hope we will use the technology on Mars to build space ships, and people, like the project survivors, will fly those ships into the galaxy." Mattson-Grimes sounded like a man who grew up with graphic novels, while his contemporaries lived for streaming multi-user games, with virtual worlds of magic and munitions. The Space Rangers represented his super heroes come to life.

"Pride," Booth said. A way to recover her influence, if not the UEC's expenses, began to take shape. Turner may be on to something.

"Wars kill people," she said. "The battles, skirmishes, and terrorism since the pandemic have killed millions. When we need a boost, we haul out a war hero, tell everyone how they risked their life to save others, give them a medal, and everybody feels good again about our efforts to unify the planet. People take pride in heroes."

"Exactly," Mattson-Grimes agreed, his head bouncing up and down like a bobble-head doll. "Hope and Pride. We spin the Space Ranger Project as a success, not a failure. Yes, people died. We lost good people from every corner of the Earth. They died because they believed in a united planet. The people of Earth reaching for the stars, as one. More importantly, a dozen lived. People will rally around them."

"Okay, Turner, I agree. But we have to do this carefully. Until it's all out there, and news people have confirmed the story, and we can honestly lie about having anything to do with the leak, we must keep this between us."

"Sure. When do you want me to start?"

"Soon, but we have to pick the right person to start with," she replied.

"No problem. I have personal, and private, connections to some talking heads at all of the major news outlets. I know we can pick the right one to get the ball rolling," he said.

"Not the right person to break the news, Turner," Booth responded. She checked her bright red nail polish for flaws. She hated flaws. She was a bit of a perfectionist. Attention to all the little details landed her in this office. She liked her office. She intended on staying for a long, long time.

"We have to pick the right survivor for them to latch onto. They come from different countries, and while all of them are tied to the UEC through their service, we need one the world can focus on."

"I get it," he replied, warming to the idea. "An icon. What's the old line? *Someone men want to be, and women want to fuck.* Sorry, no offense meant."

"I'm not easily offended," she replied. "In fact, I would love to fuck this guy." She pulled a photograph from the Space Ranger Project file on her desk, and turned it for Turner to see.

"Daniel Marcel Cooper," he read aloud the printing at the bottom of the photo. "Captain, Can-Am Army Ranger. North Africa Battalion. Why him, other than you want his body?"

"You remember the war hero we talked about? The one who gets the glory, and the medals for being, well, heroic. You're looking at him. Check your data files, Turner. Cooper has been featured more than a few times over the years. All the stories had to be written second-hand. He refuses to give interviews. He's perfect."

"Because when we leak the story, he'll continue to refuse to talk. Everyone will assume the stories are true, because he won't talk. But what if he does talk, and denies everything?" he asked.

"Not his style," Booth answered. It was all about the details. "He won't lie, and he won't talk about a classified mission. He can't talk about a classified mission. He has orders not to reveal anything about the project."

"Timing?" he asked. "Any thoughts about when we leak Cooper?"

"The people in charge are giving the survivors carte blanche. They will be able to pick any assignment, with any military unit operating under the UEC," she told the fidgeting marketing man. "Cooper isn't the type of military person who can stay away from the action. Big brass plans on using the Space Rangers for special operations, too. Something will come up soon enough, and Captain Cooper will be in the middle of it. I guarantee it."

"And when it happens, we leak the mission, and his involvement," Turner continued Booth's train of reasoning. "Someone we nudge, notices some things are unusual about the Captain. He's featured, again, as the reluctant hero, and, BOOM, he's hit with ARE YOU A SPACE RANGER AND WHY IS IT A SECRET?"

"He's put in a bad place," Booth continues, "and we, the UEC and the Board of Governors, have to declassify the project so Cooper can remain a poster boy for unification through forceful, but compassionate, methods. Our poster boy. Our hero."

"Everyone's hero," Turner amended. "He's either going to love being the center of attention, or hate it completely."

"Oh, he'll hate it," Booth said, assuredly. "I've read his files. I know this man. He'll hate it, but he'll suck it up, and keep providing us with stories. He can't help himself. He really is a hero."

END

CONVERGENCE
A Novelette In The Space Fleet Sagas

I promised something new for this collection, and CON-VERGENCE is it. This story in the Space Fleet Sagas presents the first time Space Rangers work together on a mission.

On the timeline, we are less than six months after the failure of the Space Ranger Project. Survivors have been offered any deployment they desire, so long as they keep their status as meta-humans secret, and are prepared to work for the United Earth Council when called on.

As a writer, the problem with introducing heroes with superior powers is the fear those powers will reduce the characters to comic-book status. I wanted my Rangers to have all of the advantages of strength, speed, immunity, and longevity. I also want them to be human, with the in-nate frailties and fears we all share. Some of us openly, and some of us hiding behind humor, confidence, and distance.

Here, Coop and the Rangers get to flex their new abili-ties. Will the changes created through the genetic re-engi-neering produce new personalities, or will adjustments be physical only?

DF

"We have a situation."

Melissa Booth, Canada's representative to the United Earth Council (UEC) and Director of the Board of Governors sometimes felt like every day began with those same four words. A decade since learning a weaponized virus caused the Eastern Pandemic, not a natural contagion, and she could not recall a week without a crisis.

"What now?" she asked, unapologetic for her lack of enthusiasm.

Constance Patterson, former Director of National Intelligence for the last President of the United States, held the current position of Director of the United Earth Security Establishment (UESE).

The UEC's top spy opened her data pad and flipped it around for Booth.

"These are MIRV3 reentry vehicles," a male voice, raspy and mechanical said. The video image crystal clear. "I have twelve."

The camera zoomed back, panning to show the dozen packages in two rows of six.

"These are Pre-Korean Agreement Intercontinental Ballistic Missiles. I have twelve of these," the altered voice said. "I am placing the reentry vehicles on the missiles. You will have all UEC military units depart from the Caspian-Mediterranean Corridor. I must see movement of your forces out of the region begin by noon the day after tomorrow, Tehran time."

The camera returned to the nuclear warhead delivery systems.

"I am al-Mahdi, and I claim the Corridor as a caliphate for Allah's followers. If you attempt an attack by air or ground, I will launch all twelve missiles. If I do not see an honest attempt to remove your armies, I will launch a number of missiles to prove my resolve."

The camera turned to a banner with the symbol ١٢.

"There will be no further communication. There will be no negotiation. Allah-hu-Akbar."

"Is it for real?" Booth asked.

"Weapons analysts needed to dig up some old records, but they verify you are looking at a dozen MIRV-three-dash-twelves [MIRV3-12] and a dozen Afghani-built Ababeel-class missiles. That class missile has not been used in generations, but was capable of traveling 3,000 to 4,500 miles."

Booth, former Prime Minister of Canada before the pandemic, first Prime Minister of the merged Canadian-American government, and driving force behind the United Earth Council began to feel the soles of her feet itch. A symptom of tension, and always a bad omen.

"I don't know enough to be scared, Connie. Tell me why I should be afraid of weapons decades old."

"The MIRV3 reentry vehicle holds twelve nuclear warheads. With the version Al-Mahdi has, the warheads are flight capable. The Ababeel missiles can deliver one hundred forty-four nuclear warheads to a 9,000mile diameter. Each warhead can be directed to a specific target after reentry and release."

"I'm beginning to get scared," the forty-something, open-water swimmer fit politician said. Her shoes were off, pushed aside under her desk. Toes rubbing the bottom of her right foot.

"The military expert on nuclear weapons gives a best estimate on this type of system at 250-kilotons per warhead. The disarmament agreement removed high yield nuclear weapons. It set a yield maximum of 100-kilotons for tactical nuclear weapons. The majority of TNWs are less than 20-kilotons."

Patterson allowed the fact one hundred forty-four antique warheads each packed more than twice the destructive power of any one equivalent modern missile.

"One hundred forty-four warheads will destroy a huge area, create electromagnetic interference, result in several nuclear clouds, and will kill millions of people after the initial millions killed by the detonations."

"That's the way to take me past scared to terrified," the Governor said. "So we need to bomb the crazy emir and his stash of nuclear antiques. I assume you know where they are."

Patterson continued her briefing, making sure Booth's definition of terrified was raised to a whole new level of imminent horror.

"We have a situation," Booth said to the other five members of the first UEC Board of Directors.

She recapped Patterson's brief, and waited for questions.

Besides Can-Am, represented by Booth, the Board of Governors came from Japan, the United Kingdom, Sweden, Argentina, and Saudi Arabia.

"al-Mahdi, the Hidden Imam," Omar Husam ibn Afzal, the Saudi said. "The sacrilege is evil. This person is claiming to be the Moslem messiah. Does he offer proof?"

"Proof he is the second coming of Muhammad ibn al-Hassan . . . no," Booth answered. "Proof he has nuclear missiles, yes. Will they work the way they did when built, who knows? Analysts say they could."

"The ١٢ symbol is the number twelve in Persian. Twelve MIRV3 vehicles, with twelve warheads each, and twelve missiles capable of delivering them," Booth said.

"That is not what the symbol means," Husam interrupted. "The Shia Moslems are also known as *Twelvers*. al-Mahdi was the twelfth, and last Imam. His return is suppose the mark the beginning of total Islamic dominance of the planet."

"Bomb the bastard," Teresa Watson of the UK interjected.

In response, Booth illuminated the rear wall of the Governors' Chamber. A map appeared.

"The Caspian-Mediterranean Corridor, formerly Iran, half of Iraq, and one-third of Syria," Booth said. "This Corridor was created and given to Iran for joining the nuclear disarmament agreement following the Korean incident."

"And they had to recognize the nation of Israel, which got the Israelis to sign the agreement," Takeru Sanada of Japan said.

Booth zoomed in on northeastern Iraq and the Caspian Sea.

"This is coming from Tehran?" Britta Vikander asked.

Instead of answering, Booth moved the map southeast, and zoomed in on a city covered in haze.

"Qom," Husam said.

One Hundred-twenty miles from the Iranian Corridor Capital, the old city once thrived with dozens of mosques, museums, and schools. The Pandemic, followed by riots and looting from bandits and ex-military gangs, left it covered in a continual haze of old smoke.

She tracked northeast of Qom, providing the assembled a grasp of where they were by showing Tehran and Qom first.

At thirty-five miles she slowly zoomed the satellite feed until the perspective was a couple of miles above the surface. An old installation, obviously military in origin, sat ugly and discarded next to a small desert mountain.

"Fordow," she said.

Omar Husam came out of his seat. "Fordow, the nuclear facility once used by the Iranian Space Agency. Closed three separate times in history. The Khame-Neis lusted for the power of nuclear capability. Every time they were discovered attempting to make bombs, the world shut them down."

"We have to add a fourth time in history," the Canadian said. "It appears Tehran hid high-yield nuclear tips in the mountain at Fordow. They also left a dozen ballistic missiles on site. A group of extremists led by the guy calling himself al-Mahdi is demanding control of the Corridor as his caliphate."

"I say again, Bomb the bastard," Watson repeated.

"The site was bomb-proof when it was first built, and remains that way," Booth said. "Tunnels buried inside the mountain. Reinforced concrete and steel. The warheads could be anywhere down to two hundred fifty-feet beneath the surface."

"Shoot them down when they launch," Vikander said. "We send every air-asset in the UEC military to the Corridor. When the rockets lift off, we take them down."

"Timing," Booth answered. "We have no idea when they might decide to launch. They could wait until they see an opening, or they could launch when they detect assets being deployed to the region. In fact, that was a direct threat included with the message. If we move anything towards them, they launch. If they don't see military units being removed from the Corridor by noon day after tomorrow, they launch."

"Shoot them down after they release the warheads," Vikander amended. "Use air-assets, weaponized satellites, surface-to-air intercept missiles."

"Analysts estimate with the modern capabilities we have, compared to the anti-ballistic missile defenses prior to the ban, our forces would be close to seventy-five percent effective. Thirty-six nuclear warheads representing 9,000 kilotons would reach their destinations. Plus the release of radiation in the atmosphere from the one hundred-eight we did manage to hit."

"Why only seventy-five percent?" Watson asked.

"Several factors," Booth said. "The systems also carry decoys. The individual warheads are piloted, and can avoid some of our efforts. Human error. Luck."

"You have, indeed, brought us a situation Melissa," Juan Dario Rivas of Argentina said. "I believe you have taken time to consider options. You want us to consider those options, and select one. ¿Sí?"

"We can completely eradicate the Fordow location, but we would have to go in fast with maximum force. It would mean the destruction of almost everything within one-hundred miles of the center of the installation."

"You would destroy Tehran, and Qom would be reduced to ruins," Husam said. "Qom is one of the holiest sites in Islam. Moslems would riot, and no Moslem-majority nation would remain in the UEC."

"Agreed," she concurred with the Saudi. "If we wait, it means opting for the seventy-five percent kill rate."

"Without knowing where the twenty-five percent lands?" Sanada responded. "Not a wonderful option if your family is in the twenty-five percent. Plus the fallout from the radiation. Depending on where the warheads are intercepted, winds could kill and sicken millions. Entire regions of the planet might be uninhabitable for centuries."

"Agreed," Booth repeated. "We can give al-Mahdi the Corridor."

Five voices called *NO* in a mix of languages, and some added colorful adjectives.

"Give in to a terrorist? Give in to an extortionist, and in is only a short time before they make their next demand," Husam said to the agreement of all.

"Military ground options? Special operations?" Rivas inquired.

"A force large enough to assault the installation would be detected, even with our best covert methods," Booth said, repeating what her military advisors told her. "They would have to take equipment and weapons capable of getting though an unknown number of guards, and complete force-penetration of the mountain bunkers."

"You are offering no viable options," Rivas said. "There cannot be a problem with no solution. What are we missing?"

"A covert force small enough to go unnoticed, and capable of avoiding or winning a confrontation against an unknown number of enemy combatants. Special Operators capable of gaining entrance to the fortified missile bunkers, removing barriers, human or otherwise, and then disarm or destroy the missiles before the warheads are activated."

"Something not available, or possible," Husam, a General in the Royal Saudi Air Force when not acting representative to the UEC for the Saudi Peninsula, responded.

The data-pads sitting in front of each Governor pinged. Booth linked them to hers. The lit screen displayed a cover page for a UEC **CLASSIFIED: EYES-ONLY** report.

"We didn't even get moved in."

Elena Casalobos, former Spanish Legionnaire, Captain in the Maderal Oleaga Special Operations Group, complained as she looked out the portal of the shuttle.

"Has to be something important to pull us away from Pensacola and shuttle us to Tampa without warning," Coop replied. "It was a nice bungalow, and it will be there when we get back." He squeezed her hand.

Daniel Marcel Cooper, former Can-Am Ranger captain put on a calm demeanor, but he churned inside. Following the Space Ranger Project's disastrous end, the survivors were given the opportunity to choose any UEC affiliated military or paramilitary branch. They could try any service, but they had to qualify. And keep the secrets about the Space Rangers, and the project to reengineer humans for extended space travel and the rigors of exploration.

"We passed the pre-flight training exams," she said. "I was looking forward to learning how to fly."

"Both of us. Flight school will begin as soon as we get back. This is probably nothing more than a post-incident interview. Military paperwork."

The attractive brunette, dark eyes smoldering under controlled anger, said, "Bull. The SP's pulled us out of the house like we were under arrest. No one knows anything. We get put on a shuttle designed for surface-to-space flight, with the cockpit locked and no one else on board. If you hadn't refused to get on until someone told you where we were going, we wouldn't know it was Tampa."

"I have to admit using a space shuttle to take us a couple of hundred miles across the gulf is overkill."

"Por favor, Coop. Don't use words like *overkill*."

"Well, I learn something new every day I'm with you," he said. "You're superstitious."

"Cautious," she countered. "And we are already beginning to descend."

The UEC Joint Command and Intelligence Center occupied an area west of Tampa where the United States once operated MacDill Air Force Base. The rising waters of the gulf claimed the end of one runway, all of Bayshore Blvd, and several acres of the old base. With over ninety-percent of military aircraft no longer requiring runways, the loss resulted in minimal effect on the operational capabilities of the Command.

The shuttle crossed from the clear waters of the Gulf of Mexico and settled onto a hoverport two minutes after reaching land.

Casalobos exited first, still clad in the clothes she wore moving into the Navy-issued housing. Dark blue tank top over a black sports bra accentuated the swell of her breasts. The tank, cut short, offered a glimpse of toned honey-colored abs. The form-fitted yoga pants completed the look that made an approaching Can-Am Army MP stumble.

Coop followed. Can-Am Ranger desert-sand t-shirt, black cargo pants, and laced hightop basketball shoes. He could make heads turn with his scruffy good looks, dark brown eyes, and trim six-foot-one physique, but standing next to the Spaniard he disappeared from view. At least from the view of the male MP with eyes on Elena.

The Lance Corporal came to stop and inquired, "Captain Casalobos? Captain Cooper? ."

Coop simply could not stop from taking a shot at the young corporal trying hard to appear official, in charge, and not in awe of the Latin beauty who just stepped into his world.

"Exactly who did you expect to get off of a Navy Space Shuttle landing on a secure military base at this exact time?" he asked.

"You, sir. Sorry, sir. Ma'am. Please come with me. Admiral Myerson is waiting for you."

The MP made a sharp about-face and half-walked, half-marched away.

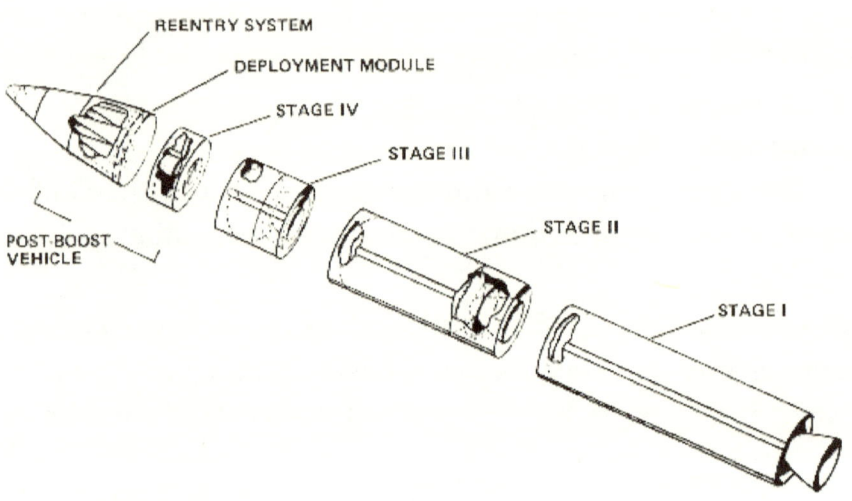

The two Captains fell in behind, exchanging a look of recognition.

Admiral Jonas Myerson commanded the military aspects of the Space Ranger Project. Practically speaking, he commanded the entire operation.

The three-story brick and stucco command center stood in the center of a sea of marble flagstone. The MP bypassed the building, crossed a street, and led them to a single-story building with no markings indicating its purpose.

The Corporal opened the front door, stood aside, and allowed the two to enter. He did not join them.

"I'm in here," called a voice. The *here* turned out to be a comfortable study with a bay window overlooking a land-scaped yard. The *I'm* was Admiral Myerson, ensconced be-hind a walnut desk placed in front of the view. His back to the window, his attention on a holo-image covering the en-tire surface of the eight-foot long, four-foot wide desk.

"Fordow Fuel Enrichment Site," he said, not looking away from the hologram. "What do you know about it?"

"Ancient history," Elie said. "Iranians used it as a secret location to enrich uranium for weaponization. The world found out and shut them down."

She and Coop stood across the desk from the Admiral. In all the time at the Project, and the weeks of intensive inter-views and tests following the death of two hundred-eight fel-low volunteers, they had never spent even this much time alone with the Admiral.

"Found out and told them to shut it down," Coop amend-ed. "No one back then believed they stopped trying to pro-duce uranium-235. The Revolutionary Guard just got sneakier."

Myerson, speaking to Coop and Casalobos as if they were old friends, not subordinates, and not, for the most part strangers, said, "The past has done more to fuck up the fu-ture than all the politicians put together."

The hologram winked out, and Myerson continued.

"Some fanatic located a dozen hidden MIRV3 capsules with multiple nuclear warheads. He has access to twelve bal-listic missiles. He wants the UEC to give him the Caspian-Mediterranean Corridor for his own fiefdom, or he launches them who-the-hell knows where."

"He's a Christian?" Coop asked.

"He calls himself al-Mahdi, the Hidden Imam, so, obvi-ously Muslim, not Christian," Myerson replied.

"Then he wants a caliphate, not a fiefdom," Coop answered.

"Cooper, every report ever written about you since you entered kindergarten includes the terms *smart* and *smart-ass*." The Admiral crossed his arms. "Do you enjoy pissing off your commanding officers?"

Unruffled by the Admiral's tone, or implied threat, Coop said, "Point one, Admiral. When you deal with enemy combatants in the Middle East, you better damn well know exactly who you face. Each religion, sect, sub-set, and tribe thinks and acts differently based on their interpretation of God's design. If the words you use are not the words used by the enemy, don't use them. Terms, phrases, and context mean as much as the actual message."

"Point two?"

"Yes, actually, I do enjoy pissing off superior officers."

Elena, watching and listening, nearly choked when Coop made the pronouncement to the Admiral.

The Admiral's grey eyes squinted, bringing the ridges lining his forehead close to this bushy eyebrows, and then he smiled.

"Yeah, me too," he said. "Only I've lived so long I'm now superior to almost everybody else in the military. You two grab a seat. We have a lot to talk about."

For the following hour Myerson laid out the situation in much the same manner Booth did with the Board of Governors. He paused when an Aide delivered drinks and sandwiches. Finally, with everything presented, he summarized the decision of the Board of Governors.

"They want a team of Space Rangers to go into Fordow and eliminate the threat," he said. "Opinions?"

Coop nodded for Elie to speak first.

"We aren't a team," she began. "Most of us barely know one another, and we haven't spent time together since you released us from Nevada. I cannot speak for the others, but I am not entirely comfortable with my new (she hesitated, seeking the right word) *abilities*."

"It's a bit alien," Coop agreed. "You think you're out for a jog, and you complete a mile in less than three minutes. You try to move a sofa, and you find yourself holding it in the air with one hand. You don't mean to do these things, Admiral. It can freak you out."

"Always having to be careful not to do something extraordinary in front of others," Elena added. "I do not know my limits. I know how much testing we did in Nevada after everything settled. I think I am stronger, faster, and have more endurance now than I did then. I do not know how I will operate within a team during a field mission."

"Elie and I have each other to work with, and sort out some of these issues. We spar. Compete to get a feel for how much we have changed. I do not believe any of the others have that kind of support. It could be, probably is, harder for them to accept the changes."

"Super powers aside," Myerson said, "are you mission capable as special operators? Do you still have the skill set to engage an enemy in the field?"

"Yes," Coop answered immediately.

"Si," Casalobos echoed.

Myerson reached into a desk drawer, pulled out two old-fashion binders with clasp-locks. He used his fingerprint to unlock the clasps, and tossed the binders in front of the two special operators and Navy pilot wannabes.

"Those binders have flash explosives in the covers," he said. "I use them because you can't hack paper, and if the wrong person tried to access the information, boom. Everything destroyed."

Coop and Elie flipped through the pages. The binders detailed every mission either ever completed. These were some of the most covert engagements by Can-Am, Spanish, and UEC operators since each joined their respective militaries.

"I don't agree with the Board of Governors that sending in Space Rangers is the only option for stopping al-Mahdi," Myerson told them. "I believe we stop him by sending in the best trained agents we have. That those operators are also enhanced is a pleasant extra benefit. It's going to take experience, instincts, brains, and the ability to make the right decisions at the right times. I think you are both qualified. What do you think?"

"Do we get to pick the team?" Coop asked.

"That's why you're here first," Myerson answered.

"How much time do we have?" Elie asked.

"Pick who you need. I'll get them here in hours, no matter where they are. Plan the mission tomorrow. Go the same night. That's all the time we have."

"We'll need all the intel we can get," Coop said.

"And a lot of coffee, espresso preferred," Elie added.

"There's more on the way."

Ensign Pamela Patterson said. "The Admiral told me to collect anything and everything on Iranian nuclear and missile programs going back to the late twentieth century. To concentrate on refinement centers and Fordow specifically, as well as photos, maps, and information regarding the area around Qom."

Myerson introduced the young Naval Intelligence officer to Coop and Elie after moving the meeting to the secure Operations and Planning Studio (OPS) located on the second floor of the Command Center building.

The sun setting on the Gulf, beautiful and brilliant on this early Florida summer end of day, passed unseen by those in the studio.

No windows, total electronic security, and guards in the hallways to protect the information and conversations of those working inside the OPS.

Massive display screens covered three walls inside the studio. Two tables with tops holo-graphic capable, ergonomic seating on silent wheels, stacks of files (dusty), and a huge coffee maker with a dozen flavor options plus teas completed the interior.

On entering the studio, the introduction made by the Admiral amounted to exactly: "This is ENS. Patterson. Naval Intelligence. Patterson - Cooper and Casalobos. Give 'em whatever they want."

Myerson departed to begin collecting the personnel Coop and Elie required, leaving the diminutive blonde in her crisp Can-Am Navy uniform standing at attention.

Breaking the ice, and relieving the tension, Casalobos offered her hand, "I'm Elie."

Patterson took the proffered greeting, her shoulders dropping two inches as she let out a breath. "Pam," she replied.

"He's Coop," Elie said. "There's a lot of things going on in here," she said, releasing the handshake and scanning the studio. Which prompted the Ensign's warning of '*more on the way*'.

"Forget the history, and let's concentrate on topography and visuals for an area fifty-miles around Fordow," Coop said. "We have to plan an incursion, Pam. Doesn't matter what is there, or was once there, if we can't find a way inside."

"Yes, sir," Patterson answered. "Everything relative to terrain, as well as everything on the actual site, compound, and bunkers, will be on your right. Current intel, satellites, surveillance, communications, news reports, personal streamers, or anything the filters pick up relative to Fordow, Qom, Tehran, the Corridor region, or al-Mahdi is collecting in the space in front of you."

"Coop, Pam. Not, sir," Cooper said.

"Coop." She said the name, let it settle, and decided she liked the sound. "And Elie," she added. She liked the names, and already liked the Rangers. A quick judge of character, she always went with her first instincts regarding people. Her mother taught her the importance of initial impressions.

"Everything else is to your left," she said, spreading her arms at the collection of real and electronic data.

"And more on the way," Elie repeated. "Pam, you think you can get us fresh clothes?"

"Sure. Give me your sizes and I'll call supply."

"Can we make calls from here?" Coop asked.

"Any screen is directly connected to secure com lines," Pam answered. "We are the Central Command and Communication Center for all branches of UEC military forces. Coms are voice activated. Your voice prints are already encoded. Just say "*COMS*," and say who you want. The better the description, like rank, full name, probable location, the quicker the connection can be made. The system will send requests across every communications possibility associated with the name. When they answer, regardless of the format, it will be routed directly here."

Coop tested the system.

"COMS. First Lieutenant Titus Andronicus Barnwell, Junior. Can-Am Marine Intelligence. Washington, DC."

Eight-seconds ticked by and the display screen in front of the three came alive with a bigger-than-life handsome African-American face.

"Cooper. Captain Casalobos," the man said. "How in hell did you get access to this channel? Fewer than a half-dozen people possess the required clearance level."

"Good to see you, Tab," Coop said. "I suppose Joint Command and Communications HQ qualifies."

"One step short of the Director for the UEC Board of Governors," the Marine Intelligence officer replied. "So this is official, top secret, and of immediate concern," he surmised. "What do you need?"

Barnwell also survived the Space Ranger Project. Coop got to know him after the program failed, and the survivors were sequestered. He liked the plain-spoken, to-the-point Marine from South Carolina the moment they began discussing options following the project.

Tab intended to return to the Can-Am Marines, and back to Intelligence. If he was not going into space, the rush he got from tracking down tidbits of rumors that helped find and stop attacks on the UEC would keep him professionally, and personally, satisfied.

"Tab, this is ENS Pam Patterson of Naval Intelligence," Coop said, introducing the two. "She will send you the parameters of the mission. I need you to go into the old Pentagon files and locate the original site details for the Fordow Fuel Enrichment Site outside of Qom, Iran."

"Pamela Patterson, as in daughter of Constance Patterson?" Tab asked.

Patterson did not answer, but did nod.

He turned his attention back to Coop.

"The location was originally a training installation for Iranian Revolutionary Guard recruits. It was also used for interrogations, prior to conversion to an enrichment factory. You want to compare the original schematics from the 1970s with what you have now."

"How soon?" Coop asked.

"Physical labor, but the human moles who care for the old files know every inch of the storage bunkers. I'm a few stories above the tunnels now. I'll get back to you within two hours," and he cut the communication.

"Constance Patterson?" Elie asked, handing Pam clothing sizes for herself and Coop.

"My mother worked in the US government, and stayed on when Canada and the United States merged," she answered, took the scrap of paper, and exited.

Elie turned to Coop, whose father served in the US Army Rangers and mother was French-Canadian. He was a military history buff, and someone who collected information and retained it, always assuming a connection in history provided insight into current affairs.

"Constance Patterson was the Director of National Intelligence for the last American President," he said. "She was also the first Director of Intelligence following the Can-Am merger. She's currently Director of the United Earth Security Establishment (UESE). She's our top spy."

"Pam has some pedigree," Elie said.

"Your father says hello."

The first mission recruit requested by Coop and Elie arrived at the mission planning studio at twenty-two thirty-one hours.

He spoke the odd greeting to Coop, then ignored him to hug Elie, now wearing desert-camo t-shirt and cargo pants delivered by Pam.

"You are still too beautiful to be with him," Anton Gregory said to her, his Russian accent slight, but obvious.

He bear hugged Cooper, also wearing Navy-issued clothing, but still in basketball shoes.

"My father?"

"I wanted to see how Can-Am Ranger training stacks up against Russian Special Forces," Gregory said. He moved to the food tray, taking a sandwich without looking, or caring what it was made from. "I asked, and was sent to the Ranger Mountain School in some impossible to pronounce place."

"Dahlonega, Georgia," Coop said.

"Nothing like the real Georgia," the Russian replied, talking around his chewing. "The Caucasus Mountains are much more impressive than Appalachians. But the women here are much more attractive. And you are?" His attention turned to the petit blonde.

"ENS Pamela Patterson, Can-Am Naval Intelligence," she replied, having not settled on a first impression of the Russian Space Ranger, other than self-confident.

"So we are going to Iran," he said. While acting at ease and unconcerned, Gregory had also taken in every aspect of the studio. "The Shia acting badly?"

While Gregory continued eating, they brought him up to speed on the situation developing in the former Persian Empire.

By the time Gregory understood the problems they faced, Tab reconnected via military satellite.

"Hello, Anton," he said. "I guess my information is worthless now. You will simply walk in and demand they all surrender."

"Which they will do immediately upon recognizing me," Anton returned. "Privet, Junior. You have information?"

"You should have it by now," the Marine said. "I digitized the files. Maps, hand-drawn site locations, photos, and descriptions of Fordow chronologically from 1970 until mid-twenty-first century. Not a lot, but it does show some details that no longer appear on more current descriptions."

"Thanks, Tab," Coop said.

"Do I get to go along?" the Marine asked.

"Not this one," Coop replied. "Special skills and minimal numbers."

"Understood," Barnwell replied. "If you can, let me know what happens." The feed ended.

"I have the data," Patterson said, holding her military-issued pad up as the studio door opened.

"I hope it includes answers," a woman said as she entered. Two men entered behind her. "No one else seems to have any," she added.

"That's why you're here, Sindy," Coop said. "To help us find answers."

Senait Kebede wore the uniform of a Major in the Ethiopian Defense Force, a military sub-division of the Can-Am Army. The EDF tasked with fighting insurgents on the African continent, providing relief to towns and villages off the normal tracks, and policing areas without law enforcement otherwise.

Her skin smooth and dark black, as were her eyes. She kept her naturally kinky-curly hair cut short to make it easier to wear the distinctive blue beret. The jungle-camo uniform could not disguise her curves. The rolled-up sleeves displayed muscled forearms. A description of her would fall between beautiful and formidable, and be exactly right.

A lanky blonde wearing a tight short skirt, with legs worthy of the outfit, followed Kebede into the room. She squealed and threw herself into Elie's arms, "Elena. I missed you, docinha."

"I missed you, too, Ali," the Spaniard replied. "It was so much fun beating up on all those men during the project."

Alessandra Campos, the only South American survivor of the Space Rangers Project came to them via the Brazilian National Security Service. One of the few volunteers who did not serve in a military or paramilitary unit. While never confirmed, most believed the rumor Campos was one of the best assassins on the planet. After observing the lithe and athletic woman in action, Coop had no doubt.

The final person through the door, a taller than average Japanese man with shaggy black hair, and a quietude of deep water. He smiled and gave Coop a slight bow of the head.

"I did not expect to be called back to your country so soon," he said. "Still, I owe a debt."

Hiroshi Kimura first met Coop and Elie during the Project when they teamed up to climb a mountain, in a lightening storm, against a clock. Hiro, former Imperial Guard for the Japanese monarchy, and Coop, lifetime marital arts enthusiast, forged a friendship while trying to best each other on the mats.

They also shared an appreciation for bladed weapons. Hiro trained in swords, and Coop deadly with knives.

Elie and Hiro worked together during the project during a simulation of a hostage rescue. The other team members stayed out of the way while Hiro downed the opposition and saved the kidnapped dummies.

When asked if she thought it counted as teamwork when only one member actually did all of the work, Casalobos replied, "Does if you have a fucking ninja on your team."

"Who else are you expecting?" Kebede asked.

"This is the ground team," Coop replied. "Everyone here is capable of stealth, infiltration, silent elimination of obstacles, handling explosives, and exfiltration under duress. We have all worked in small teams, and as lone agents. We may have to do both to accomplish our objective."

"Which is?" Ali asked.

"The elimination of twelve third-generation MIRV units, and, if possible, twelve old-style chemical-burn ballistic missiles," Coop answered.

"And a terrorist calling himself al-Mahdi," ENS Patterson added. "The mission details include capturing or killing al-Mahdi, and, if possible, discovering how he knew about the hidden MIRV3 systems."

"Secondary concern," Coop countered. "MI [Military Intelligence] always wants more intel. We stop the threat, we get out alive. Priorities one and two."

"I assume you are Team Leader," Kebede directed at Coop. "We do what you tell us to do?"

"We will need to act as a team, but we also need to be prepared to act on our own," Coop responded. "I have no ownership of this team. If the five of you would prefer someone else take command, I'm okay with that."

"But I am not."

The voice of Admiral Myerson emanated from a speaker embedded somewhere in the studio.

"This is Admiral Jonas Myerson. You may remember me from Nevada. I would be with you, but I am arranging your transportation. I am also working on providing ground intelligence and support for you when you arrive. For everyone's information, and so you understand Major Kebede, I am the commanding officer for this mission. Captain Cooper is my selection as Team Leader. There will be no votes. If you have a problem following the Captain's orders, Major, you can remain in Tampa. I will return your ass to Africa as soon as the mission is completed."

"No need, sir," Kebede responded. "The mission comes first, and I know how to take orders, sir."

"If no one else has anything pertinent to add . . . I know hyper-regenerative metabolisms allow Rangers to operate for hours on end without rest, and without a noticeable loss of performance. You should still take a break. Get some rest. MPs will show you to rooms where you can sleep, rest, shower. Please provide ENS Patterson with your sizes. Field uniforms will be delivered to you. Report back to OPS in four hours."

After a moment of dead air, Coop said, "The entire Rapid Response team does not need to take a break at the same time, Admiral. We can takes shifts and keep the mission planning rolling."

"Normally that is exactly what you would do," Myerson responded. "But I have some special items being delivered, as well as intel updates that you will need. The support teams will continue to work while you recharge."

Coop said, "You heard him. We meet back here in four hours to complete a plan. We need to be in the air in fourteen hours."

The new arrivals provided Patterson with clothing sizes, and the six left together under the care of a dozen Military Police. They walked two blocks to military housing resembling a motel. Each received a keycard to a room on the first floor. The MPs set a perimeter around the empty parking lot.

Each Ranger took note of their keycard and headed for the assigned room. Elie slipped hers into a pocket and followed Coop into his room.

Coop sat on the edge of the bed, and Elie was headed for the attached bathroom when a knock sounded. Elie switched directions, tapped the security monitor screen to life, and opened the door.

Ali Campos entered.

"The Ethiopian worries me," she said. "She obviously has issues with you, Coop. Am I wrong to worry?"

"You're right Sindy has issues with me," he said. "You have no need to worry. She won't allow personal issues to effect her field work. You can trust her to do her job, and she'll watch your back."

"Senait was assigned to Coop's rifle team in Tunisia," Elie told Ali, not asking Cooper's permission to explain the details of the *issues*. "From what little I can get out of him, they ended up having sex. Since he won't talk about it, I have to imagine it was really, really good sex. But he was a lieutenant and she was a specialist, and he was her boss, so he went boy-scout and told her no more romance."

"She felt abandoned," Ali said.

"Ethiopian girl tossed into an assignment. Alone. Insecure. Gets laid, feels loved, gets tossed," Elie said.

"Creates issues," Ali added.

"She requested a transfer, he signed off," Elie said. "Next time she sees him, he's banging me."

"Betrayed, jealous, angry, and understandable," Ali said.

"Anything else?" Elie asked.

"Do you mind if I shower here, and then join you and Coop? I'm not tired, and it might relax me," Ali said, her smile innocent.

"Not at all. The shower is this way," she said, taking the Brazilian by the hand, leaving Coop sitting on the bed, a by-stander whose opinion obviously did not matter.

"They hid a site within a hidden site."

Patterson made the announcement to the reassembled ground team. She went on to explain.

"The copies sent by Lt. Barnwell included old orbital photographs taken prior to the construction of a Revolutionary Guard training installation at Fordow. These are coordinates 34.885649; 50.99669," Patterson informed the group. The high-altitude photo displayed obviously ancient and speckled with grey and white grains. Attempts to zoom made things blend and blur into grey pebbles.

"I've time-lapsed what we have for those coordinates going back one year before construction officially began."

Ali spoke when the third image appeared.

"It is difficult to see, but are those tire ruts?" she asked.

"Glad you saw them, too," Patterson said. "Tab and I reached the same conclusion. Ten months before the site was opened to construction, trucks and heavy equipment was there. Everything always gone whenever a satellite crossed overhead."

Coop made no mention of her use of Barnwell's nickname, but did observe, "The tracks are east of the installation. On the far side of the mountain they hollowed out for the enrichment factory."

"Exactly," the Ensign agreed and continued, "the Iranians actually began secret construction on the mountain's eastern side months before overt operations on the western side. Other than building a security fence with access road for security patrols, the eastern side is never approached once work begins on the western face. To this day, no one is ever seen working on the far side. They hid a site within a hidden site."

"Edgar Alan Poe," Ali said. "If you want to hide something, put it in plain sight."

"Only in this case," Elie interjected, "hide it so when people find what they thought you had hidden, they stop looking. They concealed warheads and missiles on the eastern side of the mountain. If we didn't have these old photos, and Tab and Pam, we would only concentrate on the western side."

"When we got through the guards, breached the bunker doors, and entered the underground complex, we would have found old enrichment equipment, and little else," Gregory added.

"If the military tried to bomb the site, they would have targeted the western side, leaving the MIRV3s unharmed," Kebede said.

"Our target is the eastern side of the mountain," Cooper agreed. "Do we have any idea where the entrance is located, or how it operates?"

"We do," Pam said. She displayed four photographs of the eastern slope. "We found these in everything from official recon archives to family albums stored in the Cloud. From left to right, about ten years separates each image."

"The center left base never changes," Hiro observed. "Rocks slide, plants grow, erosion happens creating changes in the appearance of the mountainside, except a single area. It appears unchanged after forty years."

"And today," Myerson said. He entered the studio as Patterson displayed the facade over four decades. Lifting his personal pad, he swiped his fingers across the display, flicking them toward the wall. The western slope of the mountain appeared in extreme high def. The image zoomed to the left base, and the section looked exactly like it did a century before.

"You see anything else of interest, Cassel?" Myerson asked aloud.

The reply came from the screen; "One thing, Admiral." The visual swept back and forth in front of the base. "No movement in the sand and rocks in front of the camouflaged door. Either they access this side through a connection inside the mountain, or the doors open inward."

"Who is that?" Coop asked, "And is he jeopardizing the mission by being near the Fordow site?"

The camera reversed. A man swathed in traditional Middle Eastern head and face scarf smiled at the assembled with his eyes. "I am Paris Cassel. I work for UEC Security and I am over twenty-five miles from the site. The optics on this video-finder are amazing. Fairchild Industries tech, designed for use on Mars."

"Cassel is a spy," Myerson said. "He's a very good spy, and was spying on someone in the region. Director Patterson leant him to us, and I had him flown to Qom. He got where he is on his own."

"I have the other equipment you requested, Admiral, but twenty-five miles seems a long way out. It will take your team hours to get to the installation. Should I try to move closer?"

"Negative, Agent Cassel," Myerson said. "Your job is settle in and keep watch. Captain Cooper and his team will meet you there and collect their equipment."

"Roger that," the spy answered, flipping the signal back to the desert between his location and the mountain. "Whole lot of nothing to watch, and easy for someone else to see anyone coming from miles away. But it's your show, Navy. Hope to see you soon." The display returned to the linear display of four photos of the western slope.

"Any ideas yet, Captain Cooper?" Myerson asked.

"Basics," Coop replied. "We're already a small team. We break into six smaller potential targets and cross the open space as fast as possible. After reaching the fenced perimeter we reform into two teams of three. Team One finds a way to breach the western side of the mountain, while Team Two eliminates as many enemy combatants as they can, as quietly as possible. Team Two enters the mountain from the East, and locates the connector to the more-hidden side of the complex. If they cannot breach the tunnels, they create a distraction to allow Team One time to gain entrance undetected.

"Once inside, we locate, dismantle or destroy the MIRV3 components before they are set for nuclear detonation. If we have the time, we destroy the missiles. We exit and everybody heads for the rally point."

"Basic is right," Myerson said. "Any thought as to how you plan on actually accomplishing any part of your mission plan, other than the part about running through the desert?"

"The situation, and the lack of time and intel means we have to act on what we find after we are on site, Admiral," Coop replied.

"Yes, and no," Myerson said. "Tactical operations change little over the centuries. Technology, on the other hand, advances at a staggering rate. We may not have the ability to stop one-hundred percent of the multiple warheads after they deploy, but we have the ability to get you inside the mountain. It remains your job to eliminate the threat before it goes hot."

He turned to Patterson and said, "Ensign. Show them the future."

Pam directed everyone's attention to a holo display table. A three-d image of a black bodysuit appeared.

"Environmental Adaption Suit designed for use in outer space by Fairchild Industries. This one enhanced with information culled from the Martian files. It is a woven kevlar blend. The battery backpack provides power to keep the wearer at a comfortable temperature, regardless of the external temps or humidity. It also powers the suits telemetry, communications, and rebreather system."

A helmet materialized on the shoulders of the holo-image.

"The helmet seals, and you have a rebreather. You can go about two hours if necessary without external oxygen. The helmet is fully wired for communications, and provides optical advantages, like zoom, infrared, heat signature capture, and digital heads-up display. The full-front visor is coated to match the suit."

"Weight?" Gregory asked.

"Fifty-pounds with pack-battery and helmet," Patterson replied. "Half the weight without them. The kevlar and protection plates around vital organs keep the suit around twenty-five pounds. The cuffs will seal around your own boots and gloves."

She called up two holo-images to replace the suit.

"Laser side arm. Looks like an old Luger with a handle to grip, and a clip in front of the trigger guard," Gregory said.

"Powered by a crystal found in the Martian hangar," Patterson informed them. "We have to be careful with the limited supply of crystals, but we managed to build three sidearms and three shoulder-fired laser rifles. The crystals provide unlimited ammunition. You can fire laser bursts without fear of a battery dying on you. You do need to watch the heat meter on the top of the barrel. If it goes into orange, let the weapon cool for a few minutes. If it goes red, the barrel is melted and the weapon is useless."

"So we don't have to carry additional ammo, or com gear," Kebede observed. "That helps keep us lighter than the old style of loading everything on your back when going into a fight."

Pam tossed Coop a metal pen. At least, sailing through the air it looked like a pen.

"Thermaplex charge," she said as he examined the six-inch cylinder with tapered ends. He handed it to Elie, who looked and passed it along.

"The cylinder is an alloy. Inside is a thermaplex compound designed for removing boulders on Mars. Notice the red and white lines running from tip to tip. Twist the cylinder . . . no, Ms. Campos, not right now."

Ali looked up and smiled. The mischievous grin proved she had no intention of twisting the piece of metal, but only wanted to cause a bit of dark-comic relief.

"You twist the lines so the reds become one long line, and the whites do the same," Ali said, demonstrating a familiarity with the exotic explosive devise. "Place it red-side down if you want the blast directed downward, or up if you want it directed upward. Click the tip and it locks in place, even on non-metallic surfaces."

"The click also starts the timer," Patterson added. "The ones you will be issued are preset for one hundred-twenty seconds. The blast radius is actually compact, but the force is extreme. You should be safe outside of fifty-yards."

"How may pens do we get?" Gregory asked.

"The bodysuits come with loop-holders on the left and right chest. They look similar to the rifle slug carriers Cossack coats used to have. Six on each chest. A dozen, in case only one of you reaches the nuclear housings."

"And they can be used like grenades?" Gregory again.

"A very expensive, highly dangerous grenade, but yes," Pam answered. "Line up the red and white, click the tip, hold it for as long as you feel necessary, but I would not go longer than a minute-fifty, and throw."

"And try to throw it at least fifty-yards, Anton," Ali poked the Russian.

"Finally, this," the Naval Intelligence officer said, replacing the laser weapons with a tripod topped by a U-shaped barrel, traditional-looking grip, and trigger guard. A large box was affixed to the center of the tripod, below the odd double-barrel.

"A crystal-powered plasma cutter," Patterson said. "The power is strong enough to separate the gas atoms at a rate to produce a plasma stream able to cut through anything up to a thickness of six-feet, in seconds."

"Why the tripod and not hold and fire?" Coop asked.

"Backdraft," Patterson replied. "That's what the techs who came up with this version of a plasma cutter call it. The force is so strong, it will push you back, even someone with enhanced strength. You set the tripod in front of your target. Give yourself space necessary to manipulate the barrel so you can cut whatever pattern and size you require, and at least six-feet of distance so you don't get hot goo splatter."

"Hot goo splatter must be one of those high-tech terms," Ali loudly whispered to Elie, seated next to her.

"Push the set button and the tripod has a system similar to the thermaplex pens. The feet lock down, regardless of the surface."

"Sand?" Hiro asked, his first interruption since joining the team the previous night.

"I don't know if it has ever been tested on sand," Patterson admitted. "But the area around and in front of the site is compact dirt and rock with sand drifts. The feet should hold long enough to cut a doorway into the mountainside."

"Assuming we are trying to cut through a hidden entrance, and not into a solid mountain," Kebede said.

"And it is less than six-feet thick," Gregory added.

"Call up the latest satellites images for the coordinates," Coop ordered.

Patterson directed them to the display wall right.

Images zoomed to the twenty-five foot level showed a large double fence perimeter border erected around the site. It enclosed the facilities on the western slope of the mountain. Twenty watchtowers; one located every thirty-feet. Six fifteen-foot wide entry portals to the complex. Guard hut at each portal. Several buildings, the largest of which measured approximately 59,000 sq.ft.

Single fencing continued around the mountain. Only eight-feet high, averaging one-hundred-yards distance, with a one-lane rutted track running parallel and inside the aging barrier.

"The towers may have enemy combatants, but reports say they once housed Automatic Weapons Systems. Whether they still do, or if any remain operational is unknown," Patterson said.

"The enrichment facility was built deep in the mountain because of repeated threats by Israel to attack such facilities in the twentieth century. However, attacking a nuclear facility so close to the city of Qom, which is considered holy by Shia Muslims, always raised the concern of a Shiite religious response," the Intelligence Officer explained why the site remained intact.

"Anton, Elie, and Sindy will take the official site," Coop said. "Ali and Hiro will be with me on the eastern side. We meet in the middle."

"Why am I flying a bus?"

Can-Am Navy fighter pilot Rachelle Paré asked the question from the left seat of the personnel transport shuttle.

"I asked for you," Coop said, taking the co-pilot seat. The shuttle's co-pilot exited for the cabin when Coop asked for a private conversation with the pilot. The ship gained altitude as it crossed the Florida Everglades.

"We never officially met during the Space Ranger Project," he continued, strapping into the seat in spite of the ship's advanced gravitonics. Passenger and crew could move around freely inside the craft, regardless of the conditions it navigated through. Protocols did not always keep up with new technology. Flight rules required butts in the cockpit wear harness at all times.

"You always avoided me," she said. Coordinates and flight pattern entered into the flight computer, Paré turned the controls over to the autopilot. She fixed her arresting green eyes on Coop. "Why? And why am I here?"

"We met before, and I wasn't sure how to approach you," Coop admitted. "I'm not a shy person, but when I didn't take the first opportunity to thank you, I kind of kept locking up afterward."

"Thank me for what? I'm pretty sure I would have remembered meeting you. I don't."

"Shooter One," he said. "Your call sign was *Orphan*."

"Zut," the French-Canadian said, twisting to face Coop, placing the full force of her green eyes on him. "I used *Orphan* as my call sign one time. Algeria. You were the sniper on the ground calling my shots."

"And you were the renegade civilian who stole a Navy Night Eagle and saved a lot of Rangers' lives, including mine," he replied.

"So you know about that," she said, and actually broke a small smile. "I was young."

"We both were, only I would not have gotten older without your assist, so, thank you."

"Welcome. So why am I flying a bus?"

"I needed a private conversation with the best shooter in the air," Coop answered. At first, meeting her gaze proved difficult. After a few moments looking into her eyes, it would be difficult to look away. "Your call sign now is *Rain*, and you got it because troops on the ground needing air support have always used the term *call in the rain*. When you get there, you never miss."

"In a fighter, not a shuttle," she responded.

"The shuttle is to get my team to a hot zone. Bad guys have access to old nuclear weapons left over after the agreement to ban them from the planet. They plan on using them to gain control of the Corridor, or drop them, one hundred-forty-four warheads, on civilian targets. Our job is to get into a fortified bunker inside a mountain and stop the bad guys."

"Okay, tough mission. No one is calling in airstrikes, so the bunker is somewhere near too many potential collateral kills, or too fortified to take from the sky. What do you need from me?"

"I need the best shooter available overhead in case we don't get them all," Coop said. "Any missile launched will have to be taken out high in the atmosphere, hopefully after it clears the troposphere. Failing a high-altitude kill, over deep water is the next best option."

"Bring them down without releasing a nuclear cloud on the surface," Paré concluded. "I need permission."

"Admiral Myerson called Vice Admiral Murphy before you arrived," Coop said. "If you're willing to take the job, it's sanctioned."

"I want a wingman," Paré said. "Noa Tal."

"The Israeli pilot who survived the Project?"

"She's the one. I trust my guys at Fleet, but her rep and creds are top gun. She's familiar with the landscape, and also brings the advantage of enhanced skills. If we need to stay alert for a long stretch, she can handle it without drugs."

"Call Murphy and tell him to get her," Coop said, no hesitation in meeting the condition. "Tell him which fighters you need, armaments and all, for four. I want two stand-by ships capable and on hand in case anything goes wrong on your primary aircraft. Sam Harrington will be in the air as back-up in case either of you experience an airborne emergency or malfunction. As soon as you drop us off, head for Sardinia. I want the three of you over the Mediterranean Sea by the time we reach the Fordow site."

"So the bus stops in Iran?"

"No stops. Drop the back hatch when the navigation unit tells you. We'll drop from there."

"Where's there?"

"Your flight plan is for Qom's Air and Space Port, fifteen miles southeast of the city. After we jump, continue in like a normal incoming flight. After you drop beneath the scan level, veer off, stay low for at least a hundred miles, and book it back to Sardinia."

"Fifteen miles southeast of Qom," the pilot repeated. "Fordow, if I recall correctly, is twenty miles northeast of the city. You plan on a jump of forty to fifty miles?"

"Longer," Coop said. "You have to reach 40,000ft. so we have the elevation to glide the distance. Then get back down into a normal commercial air-lane before anyone picks the shuttle up on scans."

"You're making a one-hundred mile HALO, in the dark?"

Coop unharnessed and stood.

"Not exactly," he said, moving toward the cockpit door. "We aren't going to make a low opening from high altitude. We're flying in with wing-suits."

He did not wait for Paré's reaction to the incursion method for the mission. He already knew it constituted the most dangerous part of a nearly impossible plan.

The co-pilot, seeing Coop exit the cockpit, passed him as they exchanged locations.

"Everyone should have the environment suit on under your BDU," he addressed the five team members. "If you don't this may get a bit embarrassing. Strip down."

Within minutes all six stood barefoot, dressed in the tight bodysuits.

"Anton, could you pull out the packages in the overhead ben on your right?" Coop asked the Russian. "You will find six. Hand them out."

As soon as the packs came out, Gregory tossed them to the person whose name was sticky-labeled on the exterior. Rangers opened the bundles as soon as they caught them.

"Wing-suits," Elie said. "Fun."

"For you," Ali said, her face puckered, attractive even with the grimace. "I barely passed that test during the Project."

"You need to put the wing-suit on over your bodysuit," Coop instructed.

"What about the battery backpack?" Sindy asked. "And the weapons?"

"We're not using the backpacks," Coop said. "You'll each have a small battery pack, which straps onto your thigh, to power the environment, coms, and optics. Switch it on before you exit the shuttle. With the helmets on and everything sealed, you will have heat, oxygen, and heads-up displays. Maintain audio blackout."

"Weapons?" Sindy asked again.

"Waiting on the ground. Cassel will have them and a re-placement battery. We jump in [he looked at the mission recorder on his wrist], twenty-six minutes. Agent Cassel will start a homing beacon at our departure. It is on an extremely narrow bandwidth. Your helmet telemetry should be the only system on the planet capable of intercepting the ping."

"Distance?" Hiro asked.

"From the point of departure, 40,000ft. down, and one hundred-eight miles northeast," Coop said, opening his bundle.

"One - *Ohmygod* - Eight miles?" Ali, sort of, repeated.

"You nearly killed me!"

Agent Paris Cassel lay sprawled on the rocky ground.

Elie removed her helmet and asked, "You okay, jefe?"

"You nearly killed me," Cassel repeated, coming to his knees, head on a swivel, fearful of another close encounter with a silent human bat sailing in from an ink-black sky filled with millions of stars.

"You should not stand so close to the transponder," Elie answered.

"I was told your team would jump from over a hundred miles away, and from five-miles up," the spy sputtered, still jerking his head from side to side. "I expected the closest landing would be at least a half-mile away, and you would jog in, not fly in head high on the dime."

"Relax, agent." Elie set the helmet aside and began removing the wing-suit. She pealed it away from her body suit, and sat down to remove her boots to get it over her feet and off. "Everyone else is down, and will be here in a minute."

"Less," Sindy said, walking in from the East. She tossed her helmet to Cassel and began undressing. Coop, Hiro, and Anton joined them before she had the outer garment over her hips.

"You're missing one," Cassel said.

"Ali's a bit further out," Coop said. "I'm pretty sure I saw her land on her ass."

"On my ass on a fucking rock," she said, entering the rendezvous point from the Northeast. "I hate these things, and I'm going to have a purple and blue ass cheek for a week."

"You have our gear?" Coop asked the UEC agent.

By answer, Cassel headed for a beat-up all-terrain hover-rover. The rover's engine operated silently on stealth mode, and the driver could navigate solely by instruments, or with night-optics if necessary. Top speed of one-forty over badlands. He opened the back hatch and began pulling out gunny sacks.

"Three new laser rifles, and three laser pistols. One super-supreme plasma cutter, with tripod. Six battery packs, and thirty-six blow-sticks."

The thermaplex cylinders lay six to a molded foam pad, six pads deep in a metal-alloy box. He placed it gently on the ground beside the rover.

"They tell me they can't detonate if the lines aren't lined up, but I don't trust what anyone tells me," he said, explaining his caution with the box of explosives.

"Site update," Coop requested.

"No changes I can see. That includes not seeing any guard changes, and I've been here long enough for at least one rotation to have occurred. Only other issue is starlight. The moon isn't up yet, and it's only a sliver tonight, but without any humidity, there are enough stars out we don't need special optics to see each other and the immediate area."

"No guard rotations bother me," Coop said. "The star light is what it is. We'll need to be a bit more cautious approaching the targets."

"Sensors and AWS defensive systems?" Gregory mused aloud.

"Maybe," Ali answered. "Or two or three guards per watchtower taking turns without having to leave the postings."

"Hadn't thought of that," Cassel said. "There are eight vehicles inside the fences. Specs on them indicate a potential for as many as sixty-four enemy combatants."

"If they only made one trip," Hiro said.

"And didn't sit on anyone's lap," Anton added.

"Or ride on top," Elie chipped in.

"Well, intel from local villagers confirm all eight arrived together, and did not go out again," Cassel said. "Whether people sat on laps or rode on top, can't confirm or deny. They made sure they arrived when no satellites were in range."

"No point in worrying about it," Coop said. "Everyone grab your gear. Hiro, take the tripod. I've got the cutter."

"Because you don't think a girl can carry the weight and run across the desert?" Ali asked, a bit huffy.

"Because I've seen you run," Coop said. "Even with a sore butt, you're faster than either of us, and a smaller target. I want you out front with the rifle."

Mollified, Ali picked up the laser weapon and checked the action.

"Elie, Anton, and Sindy. Split up and head away before turning back and circling around to the other side," Coop said. "Meet at Elie's signal. You'll have to decide best course of action from there. By the time you get to your position, we should have the cutter set up. Elie, give me a triple tap on the com. I'll start cutting when I know you're ready to go."

"It will take at least five hours to cross the desert on foot from this distance," Paris said. "That isn't going to leave a lot of time before morning. Should I try to get you closer in the rover?"

"We'll be on site in an hour," Coop assured him. "You wait here, and if we come in hot, be prepared to lay down cover. Ali, take off. Team Two, go. Hiro, go right, and I'll come in from the left."

The six Space Rangers melted into the night, leaving a secret agent with a perplexed look. "Good luck," he said to their backs.

The telemetry display inside the helmets made it simple for Anton and Sindy to find Elie. She held a position west of the installation on a hillock created by Earth spoils; the rocks and dirt removed when excavating the underground tunnels.

The major work once done at Fordow occurred between one-hundred and two hundred-fifty feet beneath the mountain. The excavation of limestone, rock, and rubble required the over-sized front entrance. Trucks hauled the spoils to dumps like the one she now used as an observation platform. Hundreds of centrifuges churned twenty-four-seven in the lowest tunnels. The husks of machines designed to produce weapons-grade uranium probably still stood silent guard at the bottom level.

The complex sat in the saddle of several undulating hills, with the small mountain dominating the rear. The desert around the facility quickly changed from flats to dunes and wadis, which helped conceal the three Rangers' approach.

"Sixteen of the twenty guard towers are visible, and I'm not getting a heat signal from any of them," she said. "But they aren't cold, either. It's odd."

"Insulation," Anton said, turning his thermal optics on. "They lined the inside with reflective material. Someone in there is on their game." He turned his head and added, "Same with the guard huts at the gate entrances."

"We have to assume they are all occupied," Sindy said. "It will slow us down, but we will need to clear every one of them before we try for the tunnel entrance."

"That's why they did it," Anton said. "Confusion and doubt. And I can see five tunnel entrances from here. Which one do we target?"

"Dead center at the end of the dirt road," Elie answered. "It's the only one directly in the side of the mountain, and most of the vehicles are parked in front of it. Team One will be on the other side.

"There will be sensors around the outside perimeter, and the double fences may be ancient, but they will have sensors as well," Anton pointed out the obvious anti-incursion warnings.

"The other reason I picked this location," Elie said. "A good running start and a man-made ramp."

"You are joking," the Russian said. "I have only been a super human a short while. I have not actually practiced a lot with my new abilities."

"I have," the Ethiopian operator interjected. "This will be a piece of cake. I'll go first so you see the best launch point. I'll cover your jumps. Once we're all inside, I'll start clearing the guard huts and towers to the right, and Elie can go left. You're the best shot, Anton, so find a high spot and cover us."

Without waiting for a reply, Kebede rose and scurried to the bottom of the rocky slope.

"She's in charge?" Anton asked.

"She's got a plan, so I guess so," Elie answered, leaving to follow the other woman.

Sindy started running uphill as soon as the other two reached her. Both watched to see where she began her leap, and assumed she cleared the ground and fences because no alarms went off. There came no sound of a body slamming into ancient metal links.

Elie took off, with Anton close behind. They sailed through the air, one after the other, landing in body rolls and coming to knelling positions, weapons ready.

"That was too cool for words," Elie whispered.

"I admit it was impressive," Anton agreed. "I will have to practice more."

Elie triple-clicked her com.

A quarter-mile east, Coop lit the plasma cutter, which super-heated the gases inside the main connection. He pulled the trigger, and was surprised by the jolt traveling up his arms, and down into his braced legs. A beam of plasma shot forward and began melting the artificial rocks. The gash revealed the steel-alloy of a hidden entrance melting beneath the rocks. He tilted the cutter, and began drawing a line of fire up the facade.

"Impressive, but bright," Hiro said. He turned his back on the cutter, taking a defensive position to cover Coop. Ali did the same on his far side.

"This makes no sense," Sindy said over the closed com. "I've checked four huts and six towers. Not a single contact. Could they be relying completely on electronic sensors?"

"Same this way," Elie replied. "Finish your side, Sindy," Elie said, using Kebede's nickname for the first time. "We can't assume all of them are empty. Anton, you see anything?"

"What I do not see are eight vehicles," came the response. "There are six in front of the main entrance to the tunnels. I suppose the other two could be garaged in one of the bigger buildings. But no movement. No guards. No dogs. No warm bodies."

The three Rangers regrouped at the Russian's location. They stood at the T where two dirt tracks merged. The wider, firmly packed dirt road forming the T's base led to the main tunnel and the six parked vehicles.

"We clear the transports, and decide what to do next," Kebede said. The others made no verbal acknowledgement, but all three headed for the parked vehicles. They moved ahead using the jump and cover technique. One jumped ahead while two covered. That one found a defensible position and became cover. The one in the rear jumped ahead, protected by the other two. It took time, but assured a safer advance.

"Vehicles cleared," Kebede said.

"Hoods are all cold," Gregory added.

"This is getting mucho horripilante," Elie whispered.

"Creepy describes it," Anton agreed. "Maybe we walked into a zombie hideaway."

"What's a zombie," the Ethiopian asked, moving her rifle from compass point to point.

"Myth," Elie said. "You don't need to swing your head, Sindy. The helmet display will cover three-sixty."

"Myth, maybe," Anton responded. "But I have seen ancient documentary films that showed the result of zombie attacks. They eat your brains."

"You'd have to have one to eat, so you shouldn't worry, Anton," Elie quipped.

"Radiation," Sindy said, breathing the word like a soft exhale.

"That was one theory about how zombies were created," Anton said.

"I'm not talking about fucking zombies," Kebede lifted the helmet shield so the Russian could see how serious she felt the situation.

"What if the old munitions leaked, or melted, or whatever weaponized uranium does? The ones who came here to use the MIRVs might have walked into a radiation cloud. They may all be dead."

"And Team One might walk into the same problem," Elie said, quickly followed by opening a secure channel and saying, "Team One, this is Team Two. Have you breached yet?"

"Team Two this is Hiro. We are almost finished cutting."

"Hiro, we have run into no opposition," Elie said. "I repeat, not one enemy combatant. No signs of any. We think the tunnels may have lethal amounts of radiation. You need to take readings before you enter."

"Copy. Will do," the Japanese member of the team replied.

"I think the environmental suits will protect us for a little while, if there is radiation," Elie said to her team members. "Let's close the suits and go to rebreathers. The suits were designed for use off-world, so they have personal dosimeters. Activate the alert for a warning if any type of radiation is detected, and display exposure rates."

"So how do you plan on getting through this giant steel door?" Anton asked. "It is not only closed, it looks rusted shut."

"I plan on using the personnel door right there," she replied, pointing to the door beside the hangar-sized entrance, with the faded word PERSONNEL beneath a Farsi word likely translated to PERSONNEL.

"There's no dirt or debris blown up against it," Sindy noted. "Someone has used it recently."

The ebony special operator closed her visor, activated her rebreather and dosimeter, then said, "Standard close-quarters insertion. Anton left, I'm right, and Elie follows."

With no comments, no more talk of zombies, and time for action, the three put all of their skills on the line, enhanced with strength six-times normal, and twice the speed and reflex reaction time of the best special operators.

They entered a concourse. Dark. Deserted. Forty-foot high ceilings, and a floor of reinforced concrete. The optics showed four doors. One lone door to their right. Three in the rear wall: two close together on the far left, and one center.

"Center," Elie said. "Straight toward Team One."

Without any cover available on the barren floor, instead of jump and cover, they spread wide. Anyone making a surprise attack would be unable to take them out as a group.

Elie tested the door latch, and found it loose and operational. They entered using the same CQB technique to discover an empty corridor leading to another door, thirty-yards away.

They travelled half the distance when the sound of metal bars sliding into frame-holes came from behind.

"Blast door lock-bars," Anton said.

The three rushed to the far end of the corridor.

"No handle, metal door," Anton reported. "Most likely same bar locks sealing the door to the frame."

"And us inside," Elie said. "Team One, this is Team Two."

No reply. As Elie tried again, Kebede, a communications specialist during her time with the Ethiopian Agazi Special Forces, completed a series of systems checks, and a scan.

"Sophisticated deauth packet," she said. "It won't allow any of our signals to latch onto a channel."

"No signs of contamination," Anton said. "Nothing but stale air. We should save the rebreathers and the batteries in case someone tries to gas the corridor."

"I'll cover the way we came in, and you two watch this door," Elie said, moving back down the corridor. "If a door cracks, hit it hard. If it turns out to be a friendly, apologize later."

"Does anyone have a crowbar?"

Coop removed his helmet and noticed ashes smoldering on his body suit for the first time. He tapped out the small embers from the blow-back caused by the plasma stream slicing into rock and metal.

The face of the wall now included a rectangular box six-feet by three-feet. Feint yellow light leaked through the scars on the facade.

"Or anything we can use to pull with?" he asked. "We have a doorway, but we don't have a hole."

"Really?" Ali asked. "All the planning you put into this mission, and you didn't consider how to pull the block of steel out after you cut it. Men."

"Suggestion?" he asked her.

"Cut handholds on both sides so you and Hiro can drag the damn thing out," she said.

"Good idea," Hiro agreed. "Faster and smarter than us. Maybe she should be team leader."

"Who says I'm not?" the Brazilian spook asked. She looked away as Coop re-fired the plasma cutter and began carving indentations along the sides of the box.

It required total effort, and enthusiastic support by Ali, but the two meta-males pulled the thousand-pound slab of stucco designed to look like natural rock, real rocks cemented to the stucco, and steel-alloy portion of the hidden tunnel entrance away enough so they could tilt the top, and topple the block. The three of them combined to push it aside, leaving easy access to the tunnel beyond.

"Helmets and weapons," Coop said.

Ali led with the laser rifle, Hiro followed, and Coop entered last.

Century or older lamps lit a tunnel twenty-feet wide, thirty-feet high, but they could not estimate length because it ran into distant darkness. Fewer than a quarter of the available fixtures emitted illumination, and those provided a lambent, yellow-tinged glimmer.

Two flatbed railcars rested on narrow-gauge track, one behind the other. Both held mobile launch systems, complete with a missile lying sideways on the launch rails. Rails that could be raised for deployment.

"Radiation detected within the missile housing," Hiro reported. "No other radiation being picked up by the dosimeter. The area is not contaminated."

Coop disengaged his rebreather and removed his helmet, setting it on the floor. He stepped onto rungs to examine the delivery package on the railcar nearer the opening they created.

"No heat signatures," Ali said. "No life-form readings. No audio, video, or data signals. That includes no contact with Team Two."

"Someone attached the MIRV3 delivery package to the old ballistic bus," Coop informed them. He walked along the missile, from head to base. "The rocket is the Iranian version of the last Ababeel surface-to-surface long range missile developed by Pakistan. These were outlawed at the same time as the agreement to ban high-yield nuclear weapons."

"Small," Hiro said.

"In this case, my Japanese friend, size really does not matter," Ali said. Her helmet lay on the floor next to Coop's.

"Half the length of the original Ababeel, twice the range, and stealth capable. Once it launched, stealth-design made it difficult to see on old fashion radar. Probably still difficult with new scanners," she added. "You're not the only military history buff, Daniel."

"The warheads are live," Coop said, stopping at the navigation and control panel. "There is a switch for controlled flight acceptance, and it's green."

"I am not a military history buff," Hiro said. "What does the green light mean?"

"It means the warheads have hypersonic airfoils. Following suborbital release, they have limited flight capability. The warheads become drones, able to detect and avoid defensive countermeasures. A controller can remotely retarget a warhead in the air."

"So where are the other ten?" Hiro asked.

"Even more important," Ali interjected, "where are the people who set these up?"

"Team Two?" With his helmet off, Coop used the wireless mike sewn into the neck of his body suit. The miniature earbud remained quiet.

"Not going to work inside the tunnels," Ali said. "Like I said before, there's a de-authorization packet preventing any non-wired communications from accessing channels. The latest versions even work against military com bands. Someone has serious juice to get hold of one of these deauth systems."

"Most likely not a band of religious fanatics," Coop speculated aloud. "The deauth jammer may not be for us. With these systems hot, and as old as they are, an electronic signal could accidentally set something off."

The explosion shook the railcars, sent the overhead lights rattling, showered dust from the exposed mountain walls and rock ceiling, and made the three Rangers look to the recumbent missiles before releasing a collective breath.

"I thought we were dead," Ali said.

The distinctive pew-pew call of laser bursts mixed with the pop and prattle of older projectile weapons followed in the echo of the initial explosion.

"Team Two has made contact," Coop said, stating the obvious. "You two follow the sounds and see what you can do to help. I'm going to deactivate these two launchers, and try to disarm the warheads from the nav console."

"You know how to disarm nuclear warheads?" Hiro asked.

"No, but I hope the nav computer includes an off switch."

"You can read Farsi?" Ali asked.

"No."

The Brazilian placed a hand on Coop's shoulder, and being almost as tall as the North American, looked directly into his eyes when she suggested, "Disable the launcher. If the missiles cannot be fired, there will be time for someone else to disarm the old, probably unstable, most likely finicky nuclear bombs."

"I agree," Hiro said. "The fighting grows louder. I think we must hurry, Ali-chan."

Ali winked, her electric blue eyes clear, glowing with the excitement of the situation. She reached down to retrieve her helmet as she darted into the darkness following the ninja.

"Someone has been watching us," Elie said. "Watching and waiting to see which entrance we tried."

"We can't stand here waiting for something to happen." Sindy spoke from the center of the corridor where she could see both doors. Gregory leaned against the tunnel wall of exposed stone. Concrete slab had been poured for the hallway floor, steel jambs and blast doors installed, and a suspended ceiling added for lights and ventilation. Sindy, with a boost from Anton, popped a tile, and found less than a foot of space, and no exit at either end. The interior walls never updated to conceal the rough stone.

"I agree," Anton said. "I have no clue how to get out, but I agree we should."

"I have a clue," Sindy replied, and called to Elie. "I have an idea."

Elie hurried the length of the hall, reached the others, and said, "I have been trying to come up with something, and I got nada. Any idea is welcome."

"We use the thermaplex," Sindy said.

"Almost any idea is welcome," Elie amended. "We need a safety radius of fifty yards. The corridor is thirty. I measured it. Three times."

"Patterson said the explosive are directed and compact, but the force is higher than normal. We need a fifty-yard distance to protect against the blast pressure from the shockwave."

"We still do not have fifty-yards, and blast pressure can kill you dead as the actual explosion," Anton said.

"From either debris picked up by the wave hitting you at incredible speed, or by the intense pressure created by the explosion damaging your internal organs," Kebede replied.

"There is almost nothing in this corridor that will get thrown toward the other end. The ceiling tiles are so old, the pressure wave will turn them to dust."

"But to use enough thermaplex to take down a blast door built to resist explosives will generate one hell of a pressure wave," Elie countered.

"Built to resist explosives so many decades ago, those explosives are used for fireworks now," the special operator may or may not have spoken in jest. Her expression remained serious. Her point still valid.

"Built so long ago, who knows how many times this mountain has shifted, and how strong the door jambs are now. Finally, we have the environment suits and helmets. They were designed to withstand extreme pressures."

"Consistent extreme pressures," Gregory said. "This explosion will occur within a micro-moment. The pressure in this contained area will drastically alter in that compressed time."

"With us thirty-yards away, sixty-percent of the safety requirement, and on the ground. We know the force will travel up. If the pens can break the seal on the door, the opening will also relieve pressure."

"Sold," Elie said. "How many pens?"

"Eight," the Ethiopian replied immediately.

"Based on?" the Russian asked.

"Two top, two bottom, two on each side."

"Works for me," Gregory said. "Except there are three of us and we will have to click the tips at the same time so the pens go boom together."

"Six," Sindy corrected. "Two top, and two on each side. The floor is poured concrete over stone. Everything else is a single layer of limestone."

The one-hundred twenty-seconds from the time the three clicked the cylinders in unison provided time to reach the other end of the corridor, activate the rebreathers, *because oxygen would be sucked out of the space when the pressure wave rebounded*, turn off all communications, *to prevent hearing damage*, and huddle together in a corner.

It even left time to consider every mistake ever made, and regret every goal left unattempted.

The pressure wave hit them immediately, slamming the three into the stone corner. The rebound sucked them out of the corner and several feet along the concrete floor.

The thermaplex crumpled the blast door like tinfoil, and threw it, the reinforced door jamb, and several hundred pounds of mountain into the cavernous room on the other side.

The eighty-by-eighty staging area originally provided the space necessary for trucks to pull into the top level of the interior mountain facilities to drop off anything from food to rockets, and take out anything from people to refined uranium.

A bank of elevators stood along the far wall. An access garage door stood closed to the left. Two all-terrain haulers with half-tracks, closed beds, and lift gates sat center-right. Bonnets faced the closed garage door, and tailgates, down, faced a wide tunnel.

When loads became too heavy for hover-based transports to operate efficiently, half-tracks often performed work requiring the ability to handle rough terrain while hauling heavy loads.

The thermablast not only ripped off the blast door between the corridor and the staging area, the force tipped over two gravity-sleds. The ballistic missiles once on the sleds, lay on the floor. The people moving the missiles lay dead or injured.

The door itself teetered on the bonnet of the second hauler, having slammed into the driver compartment, destroying the cab, before coming to rest.

Stone, rocks, and white-hot shards of metal acted like shrapnel, tearing into or bowling over another dozen of the newly located enemy, killing most or causing injuries severe enough to cripple.

That left between twelve and twenty armed terrorists shaking off the effects of the explosion, concussive wave, dust and debris, along with the loss of lighting. Team Two came through the gaping doorway.

The suits protected them, and their enhanced genetics allowed them to recover faster than those left alive outside the corridor. No heat-masking fabrics kept the sensors on the helmets from outlining targets. The headlights and running lights of the haulers, dim in the choking limestone dust, provided enough illumination for the night-sight optics to provide a visual of the kill zone.

Laser fire dropped eight enemy combatants before the others began returning fire. Wild and unaimed return fire, but still deadly dangerous in the confined area.

Elie jumped a brick and mortar wall originally built as a decorative planter box. It provided a barrier against incoming high-velocity projectiles from personal weapons. Anything large as a 20mm slug would punch through the half-wall. So far, no one fired anything close to that size.

Sindy slid behind a boulder the size of a sofa. Whether it was torn from the wall because of the blast, or dropped from the ceiling a century before made no difference. It provided cover, and she could fire the laser rifle from either side or across the jagged top.

Anton remained at the doorway. He stayed behind the ragged doorjamb, picking targets with both the heat sensors and night-vision. He could also watch their backs, assuring no one surprised them by coming through the corridor behind them.

Outnumbered, the Rangers held the advantages of superior weapons, and the ability to acquire targets in the gloom. Their advantages dwindled when a dozen reinforcements arrived from the wide tunnel where the missiles were apparently hidden.

Four satchels sailed through the air, hit the concrete floor and burst into plums of light that quickly settled into a constant illumination. The battlefield lighting transformed the darkened staging area from pitch black to dusk.

"Evocation battle lights," Anton told the others over the team com.

"Hey, we have sound," Sindy replied. "The deauth must have been damaged by the blast."

"And they have light, and numbers," Elie said. "The temperature from the evocators also screw with our heat signature optics."

On cue, having more guns for support, and able to see, the enemy agents opened fire, this time directed at three hide-y-holes and not sprayed randomly.

"I didn't plan on Space Rangers."

Coop reacted immediately to the voice. His improved reflexes did not prevent the laser from cutting across his right hand, burning the skin, muscles, and nerves. His pistol fell from useless fingers.

As he worked on the wiring for the second launcher, simply ripping anything exposed away from connections, he remained aware of the opening to the desert, and the corridor Hiro and Ali disappeared down. He did not worry about the closed end of the wide hall behind him. He did not hear the hidden panel slide away, or the person step into the space he was least concerned about.

"I expected to have, at minimum, another fifteen hours before the UEC could mount any kind of planned incursion to retake the site."

He shot Coop in the left leg, above the knee.

Cooper went down, trying to take the brunt of the fall on his right knee. He did not scream, even though the laser acted like a white-hot poker stabbing into his quad.

Another shot destroyed the battery pack strapped to the damaged leg. Any thought of calling for help gone with the power source.

"Rolf Berkel," Coop said the name through clenched teeth. "You're one of us, Rolf. One of the twelve surviving Space Rangers. What the fuck are you doing?"

"At the moment, enjoying taking down the exceptional Daniel Marcel Cooper, the best the Can-Am Rangers could offer."

The laser cut across Coop's left shoulder, causing pain, but little damage. The same burst cutting through skin and bone, cauterized the wound, preventing bleeding. Berkel might cut him into pieces, but at least he would not bleed out. Tiny favors.

"Always coming out on top during every test. Always in bed with the hottest woman. Always the winner, and that before the genetic enhancements. I got so tired of people kissing your ass, I researched you, *battle field-commissioned officer* Cooper."

Coop called on his new strength to push the pain away. He needed his improved speed to cover the distance and take the German down before he could . . .

The shot cut into Coop's right thigh. This time he cried out in pain and frustration as he dropped.

"I'm enhanced, too, Cooper. I have the speed, strength, and reflexes to match yours. Plus I'm smarter, and I have a weapon. Nice, isn't it. Integrated phase array to prevent blooming. Makes it extremely accurate at short distances."

"Why?" Coop asked.

"Money, dummkoft. I was hired to retrieve ten ballistic missiles and ten MIRV3-12 warheads. I knew the attempt to recover the hidden cache would be noticed. The whole *al-Mahdi* bit was to give me the time to dig them out, load them up, and disappear before military units could move in. As I said, I did not expect the UEC to use Space Rangers this soon after the project shut down."

"Ten."

"Yes, Captain, please try to keep me talking until help arrives, or you figure a way to beat me," Berkel said, placing a laser through Coop's left biceps.

Already on his knees, the pain from the wound sent his forehead to the ground.

"Supplication," Berkel said of his prey's position. "These two are my cover. Once the trucks were loaded and ready to go, I was going to launch these two. While everyone panicked, I would drive to a location near Qom and transfer everything to a waiting shuttle. I figured one aimed at Rome and one at Jerusalem would shake up the UEC."

"Only one now," Coop said, raising his head, managing the pain.

"As I said before, I researched you. Father a Colonel in the Rangers, commander of the Mountain Training facilities, and you an enlisted soldier. Serious pride issues there, Captain. Plus getting your team, including your best friend, killed in Egypt because of your lack of experience, and failure to act decisively. Anyone else would have been kicked out of the service. You, Daddy's boy, got another chance. Got a field commission because all of the officers on the mission were killed."

Coop tried one more time to summon the will to attack. The laser took him in the abdomen, cut through the lining of his stomach, and exited out his right side. The pain and shock so great, the breath ripped from his lungs. He could not scream. Falling forward, he twisted to land on his side.

"I did not expect you, or the others, but I knew I would one day face you. I knew I would beat you. You are overconfident in your skills, and while you pretend to care for the others on your team, you always abandon them. When I recognized who the UEC sent, it was just a matter of waiting until you were alone. You always work alone, Cooper. You always turn your back on the team for personal glory."

The German turned his back, showing his contempt for the disabled and beaten adversary.

"I'm a mercenary now. When I realized the gift I received by surviving the Project, I also realized the potential for profit. They offered us service in any branch of any military unit. Fuck them. I serve me."

Coop tried to focus. His vision, blurred by tears and hampered by the dusky light of the corridor, made the German a shadow against darker shadows. He watched as Berkle opened a panel on the corridor wall.

"The launchers use independent power and control systems when they are outside," he said. "When inside the complex, a different system is in control. You accomplished nothing by ripping away wiring. It did provide the distraction I needed to ambush you, but nothing more. All I need to do is press these two red knobs. Everything necessary for launch to delivery has been pre-coded into the system, the missiles, and the individual warheads. I push the red knobs, and the remainder of the portal you cut through opens, the launchpads lift and pivot the missiles, and they are sent on their way."

Berkle walked back to Coop. Realizing his enemy and fellow Space Ranger Project survivor had nothing left to fight with, he came close enough to grab Coop's sweat-wet hair.He pulled it back until the injured man had to look the German eye-to-eye.

"Rome. Specifically Vatican City, because it will shake the Catholics. Jerusalem because it will devastate Christians, Jews, and Moslems when the Temple Mount and nearby holy sites are vaporized. We are sending a message. Faith is worthless. The UEC is impotent."

He placed the tip of the laser pistol in front of Coop's face where he could see the final burst.

"You, because I can."

"Tenno Heika Banzai."

Hiro exited the tunnel first, his war whoop startling a shooter preparing to fire a .50 mm rapid-fire machine pistol into Elie's location. Hiro's shot followed his cry, stopping the shooter before he could chew up the bricks and the woman knelling on the other side.

The blade in his left hand sliced through the back of the neck of a female terrorist using rifle fire to force Elie stay behind the wall. Her plan was to keep the Spaniard in place until her companion finished her off. She died unrewarded.

He kicked the next killer in the back of the knee, drove the knife into his skull with enhanced strength pushing the long blade though the thick bone. The next two laser bursts took out one combatant shooting from behind a hauler's half-track, and one firing at Anton's position from behind one of the fallen missiles from the grav-sled.

The remaining gunners, realizing another player had entered the game, turned to fire on the rapidly advancing Japanese Ranger.

Ali came into the staging area with her laser rifle already up. She triggered one burst after another, keeping ahead of Hiro, killing some, and causing enough disruption so those she could not target hesitated long enough for the ninja to take them with his pistol or blade.

Once Anton, Sindy, and Elie realized they were no longer being suppressed, they rose from protection to add their firepower.

In less than sixty-seconds, the combined efforts of the two teams eliminated every threat. Without comment or command, the five investigated the area, assuring it clear of potential threats.

Anton and Sindy used plasti-alloy ties left lying on the floor to strap the hands and feet of wounded enemy fighters. The ties, normally used to secure items in the haulers, were dropped when the initial blast sent a shock wave through the staging room.

They did not have the medical supplies, nor the inclination, to aid the wounded.

Ali removed her helmet and said, "It is so much nicer being the hero."

"Where's Coop?" Elie asked.

"Relax, bombom," the former assassin turned hero said. "Your boy is making sure two missiles we found can't be used."

"He doesn't answer," Elie said, trying to call Coop through the embedded mic on her suit collar.

"He was not wearing a helmet," Hiro said. "He also thought a stray signal might accidentally set off the old weapons' control systems. He may have his personal coms turned off."

"Coop will join us as soon as he can," Anton said. "We need to set a perimeter, and someone needs to contact Cassel to call in reinforcements. I suppose we should request medics."

"I'll make the call from the main entrance," Sindy said. "It's the closest exit, and once out of the mountain the signal should have no problem getting to Cassel."

"Elie, check the first hauler. Make sure there are no terrorists hiding in the back, and the weapons loaded are dormant," Anton said. "I will check the one with the new hood ornament. Hiro, keep an eye on the elevators and the wounded. Ali, make sure Coop is the only one coming out of that tunnel [indicating the corridor she and Hiro emerged from minutes earlier]. Sindy will have the other entrance covered while she calls the spy."

No one questioned Anton issuing orders. Each time a situation called for a team member best suited to assume control, it happened organically. Anton had the most experience as a ground force commander.

"When the haulers are cleared and Sindy returns, you can go help Coop," he told Elie, who nodded in agreement, understanding the priorities.

Ali, bending down to recover her helmet, hesitated. A life as a covert operator and silent assassin honed her ability to listen and identify sounds. Her acute ears saved her life more often than the weapons she carried.

The sounds coming from the darkness faint; barely conveyed from far away by the acoustics of the tunnel. Weak, but recognizable.

"UGH!"

Ali slammed into the middle of Berkel's back, her speed adding force to the body-blow, sending them both airborne.

His reflexive pull on the trigger sent a laser burst through the plasma-cut opening, arcing harmlessly into the night. The power of the tackle would have snapped his spine before the genetic reengineering of his bones.

He hit the concrete floor first, cushioning her landing with his body.

She rolled off, onto her knees, and quickly to her feet. In her hand the fighting knife she always carried, pulled from its calf sheath. The blade made from heat-treated high carbon blued finished steel. Razor sharp and ready for work.Unlike the composite handles favored by military operators,her favorite weapon used a round contoured close-grained hardwood handle with 4 grooves. In her hand, it became part of her.

Ali did not recognize the German until he moved impossibly fast, recovering from the crushing blow, tumbling away from her slash, rising with his own knife in hand. The tantō-style dagger made of black stainless steel with a polymide handle designed for use by the left or right hand. She recognized the knife first.

"I knew you were a piece of shit, Rolfy."

"Alessandra. My teammate from the close quarters combat drills. If killing Cooper is dinner, you are dessert."

She took his moment of gloating to close the distance, a flurry of slashing attacks at his face and neck.

The former KSK (Kommando Spezialkräfte) lieutenant used his training and enhanced speed to counter the knife strikes. Ali's blue steel blade sparking time after time against the German's blackened steel.

Ali had the advantage of time spent sparring with Elie and Cooper. She even managed a couple of advanced lessons from Hiro. These sessions followed the changes. She had gone against genetically enhanced opponents. Berkel never mixed well with others. Any practice since becoming a meta-human would have been against normals.

She pushed her advantage, mixing kicks with thrusts and slashes of the knife. She pressed Berkel back; keeping him constantly on defense.

Initially awed by the speed and ferocity of her attack, he quickly adapted. He controlled his breathing. He watched Ali's patterns, staying just out-of-range of her long arms and longer legs.

He hated Coop for being sickeningly good. He hated Campos for refusing his advances during their time in Nevada. His hatred for most people began as a coddled, entitled son of an army Generalmajor. His distaste matured while in college, where he learned how to covertly spike the drinks of women he wanted to fuck, and hide his sociopathic nature.

He accepted a commission in the Bundeswehr, where his eerie calmness under stress caught the eye of the Rapid Forces Division. His ability to lead and fight without remorse, his only concern winning, quickly led to his assignment with the KSK. They appreciated his anti-social tendencies, and improved his ability to kill.

The KSK liked him so much, his commanding officer paid a psy-ops specialist to answer the Space Ranger Project's questionnaires, assuring Berkel's questionable psychology would not prevent his potential acceptance.

Alessandra grew up poor and beautiful. A dangerous combination. As a teenager she learned to use a knife to defend herself, but only after being raped by more than one bastard attracted to the blue-eyed, blonde.

After discovering an affinity for blades, she never went anywhere without one. She never again had sex unless it was her choice.

School never seemed a viable option for Alessandra, so she supported herself and her family working for criminal gangs in Sao Paulo. Her work caught the attention of local law enforcement. They could never prove anything, despite knowing who she removed for pay.

Their reports, and her reputation eventually reached the head of Brazil's counterintelligence agency. Recruited at sixteen for money, amnesty, a safe home for her family, and the promise of sanctioned assassinations. Alessandro was given the name Campos, for her work outside legal lines.

At the Project, she recognized Rolf Berkel as the exact type of garbage that ruined her youth. She avoided him, turned away his advances, and watched her back whenever he was near.

The two polar opposites squared off; the dark-haired, light-skinned European facing the blonde, honey-skinned South American.

Cooper, fought to remain alert, trying to will his faster-than-human regenerative and self-healing enhancements to perform a miracle. He lay prone on the cold and dusty floor, a silent observer.

The fight occurred at speeds only Space Ranger Project survivors could perform. Ali, true to her nature, attacking. Ferocious, snarling, with her Latin blood boiling in rage.

Berkel remained on defense, thrusting with the knife, or kicking out offensively only to maintain separation. He remained calm, unemotional, and distant even as the Brazilian's blade slashed through clothing, biting into skin, as her attack backed him against a rough stone wall.

With her opponent unable to continue moving away, Ali feinted a knee ram to his mid-section. Expecting him to block down with his forearms, and twist to protect his groin, she followed immediately with her real attack, a killing under-hand thrust with the tip of the blade aimed at his exposed throat.

She used a similar combination twice in the short confrontation leading up to this moment. Twice she tipped the move by pivoting on her left forefoot to provide angle and power for the knee, and crossing her left arm at her ribs for balance. The two set-ups designed to add momentum to the delivery of the thrust.

Berkel recognized both tells. When the knife came, he moved in a different direction than Ali anticipated. Her knife missed him, the force driving it into the solid rock wall, the contact breaking the tip of the steel blade. Open and off balance, she could not defend against the German's black steel. His seriated blade ripped into her abdomen, the small, deadly teeth beneath the sharpened metal tearing the incision open as he yanked it out.

Coop, painfully rising to his knees, screamed profanities at Berkel. His voice quickly going hoarse from the effort.

Berkel hooked a solid punch into Ali's jaw, using the handle of the knife to intensify the strike, sending her the rest of the way to the ground, her hands clutching her middle, trying to stop the bleeding.

The mercenary ignored Coop's change from invectives to imploring mercy. He recovered his pistol, returned to the woman lying in a growing pool of blood, and lifted her by the blonde hair stained red.

Holding her against his chest, facing Coop, he raised the pistol to her temple.

"Don't do it, Rolf," Coop pleaded. "She's out of the fight. There is no reason to kill her."

Ali, face bruised, covered in blood and sweat, smiled and winked at Coop.

"You're right," Berkel said, and pulled the trigger.

The beam cut a hole through her skull, the heat melted the blue eyes, and her body crumpled when the killer released his hold.

"But I will, because I can," he said, still holding the pistol head high.

He did not see Ali kick her knife to Coop when she winked.

Driven by adrenaline-fueled rage, Coop picked up the knife and threw it in one motion. Her broken blade buried itself to the wooden hilt in her killer's throat, cutting off his self-appreciation. Her knife her vengeance.

Spent, Coop collapsed to the floor once more.

Berkel pulled the knife from his own neck, blood gushing from the wound. Wide-eyed, aware he was mortally wounded, the sociopath still did not panic. With halting, labored steps, he went for the open panel.

Disbelief and desperation were all that remained for the American. Too drained and too injured to stand. Too angry to pass out.

He watched the German's final effort, falling forward, hands up, palms out. He saw the red knobs pushed by a dead man, and heard the mobile launchers turn on. He closed his eyes and accepted escape from the pain.

"Fucking deadweight!"

Coop drifted up, awoken by the rumble of the steel door on the side of the mountain opening. He expected to see the corridor, the launchers, and Ali's body. Instead he realized he was looking from the outside, back toward the mountain.

Someone held him under his armpits, dragging him through the sand, his heels leaving wavy tracks.

"Wait," he said. Not sure he said it aloud, he said it again.

"If I wait, a mountain comes down on us," Cassel said.

"Damn it, Cassel. Stop. You have to get my helmet."

"Really?" The spy released the Ranger, who dropped like a stone, his head landing on soft sand.

"My coms are special," Coop tried to explain. "Missiles launching. Nuclear. Need my helmet."

To his credit, Cassel did not continue to argue. The young agent took off. Coop propped himself on his right elbow, the left arm too injured to hold his weight.

Cassel ran through an opening created by the huge door swinging out. The old motors and gears still strong enough the move the door and push aside the piece Coop and Hiro pulled out earlier.

He reemerged, helmet in hand. He placed it in Coop's lap, grabbed him under the arms and across his chest. The spy began hauling him away once more, digging hard for distance as loosened rocks fell ran down the slope of the mountain, dislodged by the opening door.

"Ali?"

"Dead," Cassel answered between gasps.

"Paris, stop. Please, I'm going to pass out, and you need to hear this."

"Where is Ali?" Elie asked, having cleared the first vehicle.

"She was there a few minutes ago," Anton said, jumping from the bed of the second hauler to the concrete floor.

Hiro, busy trying to makeshift bandages to stop the bleeding of two of the downed enemy, looked up and shook his head. He had been involved with helping the wounded and watching the elevators.

Sindy returned through the blasted opening. "I got Cassel. He was already on his way in with the rover. Said something about seeing a laser cut into the sky and took it as a signal. Where's Ali?"

The rumble of the mountain shook dust and debris from the ceiling. The four Rangers reached for weapons, and grouped near the tunnel entrance Ali had been guarding.

"Any ideas?" Anton asked.

No one answered, but Elie kept calling for Ali and Coop.

"We have to get down there," she said to the other three. "Something is really wrong. I can feel it."

"Helmets on," Anton ordered. "Check your weapons, and turn on optics. Check coms to make sure the deauth did not come back on. Do these, and we go."

"Hello, Hello. Copy. Anyone? This is Cassel. Anyone hear me?"

The voice came across all four helmet speakers.

"That's Coop's channel," Elie said. "This is Casalobos. We hear you, Cassel. Do you know where Coop and Ali are?"

"Yes. Coop says you have to get away from the tunnel. The tunnel with the missiles."

"Agent. Calm down and make yourself clear," Gregory ordered, his voice calm, but commanding.

"Yes, sir. Two missiles are about to launch. Coop and Ali could not stop them. The blowback will be forced down the tunnel. If you are in there, you need to get out. Now. Launch is imminent."

"Go,"Anton ordered, leading the way toward the main corridor and the fastest exit.

"The wounded," Hiro yelled, heading the opposite direction from safety.

"Fuck," the Russian replied, but changed direction, following the Japanese, the two women already on Kimura's heels.

There were five wounded, bound hand and foot. Anton picked up two, each of the others threw one over a shoulder. Still following Hiro's lead, they ran away from the exit toward a door beside the elevators. Hiro, first there, turned the knob and shouldered the rusted door open. Sindy and Elie hurried through the opening. Anton needed to stop, hand one body to Hiro, who placed his load on the landing inside the stairwell to take the one from Anton.

The Russian, able to pass through the doorway with only one person to carry, did so with great haste.

The door closed behind him, the noise from the approaching back-blast of the twin launchers firing in unison screaming towards them.

Hiro glimpsed the emerging flames as he slammed the old metal door into its jamb. Anton joined him to help hold the portal closed, neither trusting the ancient lock.

"They would not have done the same for us," he said to his Oriental friend.

"That is why we are better people," Hiro replied, the door waffling beneath his and Anton's weight, the metal noticeably warmer.

"That's what Ali said," Elie stood on the top step of the stairs. The only light in the tight space provided by their helmets. "It is so much nicer being the hero."

"Perhaps," Anton replied. "But so much more difficult."

At the eastern facade, moments after the hidden door stopped moving, the sound of gears churning under strain began as the launch pads repositioned the missiles.

"The Rangers inside got the message," Cassel told Coop, only Coop lay unconscious.

Remembering the hurried instructions, the spy spoke clearly into the helmet. "Rain? If someone called *Rain* is listening, this is UEC Security Agent Paris Cassel speaking for Captain Daniel Cooper. *err* . . . over; copy."

"This is Rain," came the reply. Female. "Where is Cooper?"

"Out of action," Cassel answered. "He told me to tell you Rome and Jerusalem. I'm sure it's related to the fact two Afghan Swallows are about to launch, and they each carry MIRV3 packages of twelve warheads. Copy?"

"Copy. Rain, out."

The roar came before the flames, giving the agent a second of warning. He used the time to throw his body over the injured Cooper. His eyes closed, holding his breath in anticipation of a horrible death by fire, he did not see the two antique ballistic shoot across the desert floor, angled to the star-filled sky.

The majority of the back-blast, heat, and destruction stayed within the tunnels, leaving Cassel and Coop untouched.

Inside, Ali Campos' and Rolf Berkel's cremated remains mixed with the dust and ash.

Checking first to assure himself Daniel Cooper continued to breath, Cassel rose and sprinted to the hover-rover parked well to the south of the mountain's base, out of harm's way.

He activated the homing beacon. Then he booted the surface-satellite communication array.

"This is Tower [his designation for the mission]." The use of his codename would route his message directly to the command center in Tampa, Florida.

"DC down. I need medical stat. Beacon lit. One more KIA. Four unaccounted. Two birds in flight. Rome and Jerusalem. Enemy reported eliminated, but not confirmed. Sweep requested. Tower, out."

Without an audience to watch or listen, the French-Canadian secret agent did not play the less-than-confident part of a raw field operative. He left the field medical kit in the rover, taking a laser pistol instead. He had no idea what to do for wounds already cauterized and closed. If Cooper had terminal internal damage, he was out of luck.

"I'll take the one headed for Jerusalem."

Noa Tal, former Israeli Defense Force AirGuard Pilot, and recent Space Ranger Project survivor called her intention to the second fighter cruising at 200,000ft above the surface of the planet.

At fifteen-miles above the planet surface, the Navy's latest fighters, Space Hawks, operated with a compact version of the ionic-sublight engines used by surface-to-orbit shuttles. Below 160,000ft the pilot could switch to twin-jets built to power the craft to a screaming Mach 4; 3,069.08mph.

"You do and they die," Paré responded. "The distance to Israel is less than 1,000 miles. The missile will not go high enough so it can be destroyed in the mesosphere, and there is only one body of water deep enough between Fordow and Jerusalem to drop a nuclear bomb."

"The Dead Sea," Tal said. "You're the better shot," she admitted. "I'll take Rome."

"Sabre [Tal's callsign] has Rome. Rain has Jerusalem," the lead pilot confirmed. "Sam, follow Sabre."

"Copy," came the reply from their back-up. No other comments and questions. Sam Harrington did not talk much, but the Royal Air Force aviator would be ready to step in if needed.

"Sabre, Rome is two-one-eight-eight miles. Intel reports these missiles have been in storage for decades. Yours may or may not apogee as high as the mesosphere. Regardless, you have to take it when third stage boost terminates. Following the third stage, it deploys multiple warheads heads on Rome. If they deploy, you and Sam combine to take as many out of the air as possible."

"If I miss it high, I still have the Aegean and Adriatic seas," Sabre replied.

Sam keyed "Copy."

"Don't miss," Rain ordered. "I have plumes. Rain, out."

During the conversation both fighters worked down towards the 160,000ft level. When Rain entered the first whiff of stratosphere, she switched to jets, sealed all ports for improved aerodynamic flight, raised and fixed her dual tail, and punched her ship towards Earth.

She had the daunting task of getting to the surface, catching a missile traveling at supersonic speed, and determine a way of bringing it down in a body of water 1,000ft deep, but only thirty-miles wide at the estimated point of over-flight.

Sabre engaged jets and flew to 150,000ft. The second Swallow (The translation for Ababeel) flew a course straight toward her.

The pilot-plane integrated helmet provided everything she needed to watch the progress of the MIRV3-12 rocket delivery system. She could even request visual, and the helmet would treat the cockpit like a glass ball, showing her every angle from exterior cameras.

Concentrating on the altitude numbers, she watched as the Swallows initial launch booster disengaged one minute after leaving Fordow.

The Space Hawk veered north, Sabre adjusting for the flight of the missile as it adjusted to the angle required to attack the Vatican.

At two-minutes the third and final stage booster motor kicked in. She wondered about Rain's progress, but did not take her focus from the Rome-bird to check. If the third stage motor, ancient and left unattended for decades, could not lift the warheads above the mesospheric line, she would be forced to follow the missile towards Italy.

One-hundred seventy-two seconds after launch, the third stage motor quit. Separation left the post-boost vehicle at 163,944ft. Depending on the location, the mesosphere began and the stratosphere ended at thirty-one miles. The MIRV3's on-board nav prepared for re-entry. Deployment of the twelve warheads could occur at any point after the vehicle reached the stratosphere.

One target at the edge of safety, or twelve nuclear pigeons scattered over Asia and Europe?

The Space Hawk's munitions included four air-to-air guided smart-missiles attached to hard-points. Two under each wing. Sabre sent all four at once, lighting the missile for the homing systems to lock onto.

Not sure what effects twelve nuclear bombs going off at once might cause, she banked her fighter port and straight down, kicking in both jets at full throttle.

The G-forces almost knocked her out in spite of the flight suit and the cockpit's protection against Hi-G blackouts.

At 3,000mph when the MIRV3 detonated, she was thirty-three miles away, pulling back the power, and trimming her flight package to follow Rain to Israel.

The rainbow effect of the nuclear warheads exploding in the high atmosphere went unseen. The electro-magnetic pulse (EMP) did not. Communications, weather, and military satellites in the immediate area all went off-line.

The command center in Tampa recorded the hit by Sabre just before everything went black.

The Jerusalem MIRV3 needed to travel a disturbingly short 976 miles. One-minute following launch, the stage one booster disengaged, and the Swallow turned into a quasi-ballistic missile.

Remaining at 10,000ft, the missile's rockets pushed it to Mach 2. It would reach Temple Mount in twenty-eight minutes. It would reach the shore at the North Basin of the Dead Sea in twenty-six minutes, and be over water for sixty-seconds. Only half that time over water deep enough to contain the fallout from a nuclear detonation.

At Mach 4, plus everything more she could pull from the Space Hawk without blowing the engines, she pursued the target from 20,000ft.

She dropped her missiles over the western desert of old Iraq, knowing less drag would give her a little more speed. She would not be using them on the Swallow. If the warheads detonated above ground, the results would be catastrophic.

Had she caught the vehicle while it was over the almost life-less desert, she might have considered the option. With the MIRV3s crossing into Jordan, too many lives would be lost with missile-on-missile.

The Space Hawk dropped from 20,000ft to 12,000ft, and Mach4+ to Mach 2 when Paré caught the ballistic missile over Madaba, Jordan and matched its pace.

The two super-sonic aircraft shook the town, loosening mosaic tiles in the Church of the Virgin Mary. People on the ground watched in awe, dumb-struck by the chase.

Ten miles and seconds to the Dead Sea, Paré earned her callsign. Without computer-tactical assist, fearing a delay as the system tried to adjust for conditions, trusting the visuals in her helmet and the steady thumb on the button, she fired air-to-air lasers.

The lasers sliced into the Afghani-designed delivery vehicle, cutting the nosecone and first compartment away from the navigation-booster sections. The shot made more remarkable at 1,500+mph.

The nose and warheads fell away from the vehicle. Rain banked, circled, and kept an eye on the dangerous portion of the package as it tumbled to the salt sea below. The warheads might still deploy, leaving her to chase twelve deadly drones.

Without the nav-system for guidance, the nuclear delivery systems never deployed. The dissected section hit the surface of the Dead Sea. Impact did not cause a detonation. The high saline content of the world's largest salt lake kept the compartment afloat for a few moments longer than comfortable, but the weight of the solid nosecone, metal compartment, and warheads finally overcame the buoyancy of the water. The MIRV3 reentry vehicle, and the deadly load it carried, sank 820ft to rest on the seafloor until a UEC recovery team could recover and dispose of the ancient armament.

The navigation package and rocket boosters overflew Jerusalem, creating a stir of excitement as the damaged missile lost altitude and speed. The harmless portion of the missile crashed into hills twenty-miles east of the city, outside the pre-biblical town of Bet Shemesh.

Sabre and Sam rejoined Rain over the Jordan-Iraq border. The three did not bother with self-congratulations, intent on returning to Fordow and a sit-rep on the team on the ground.

"You look like shit."

Anton Gregory sat in a chair against a wall.

"Thank you," Coop answered from the hospital bed.

"Pazhalooysta," the Russian replied.

"I think you look wonderful," Elie said, standing beside and above the patient.

"I think this room is too crowded," commented an older woman in a traditional white coat.

"Dr. Bright," Coop recognized the doctor from the Space Ranger Project.

"Glad to see your memory is functional," the pale-skinned medical research specialist said. "Myerson flew me in since your physiology is rare and confidential."

She activated the bed's motor, raising Coop to a seated position. Once up he saw Hiro standing beside the doorway. He smiled and nodded. Sindy sat on the window ledge.

"You're in Kuwait City, the nearest military hospital with the facilities to treat you," Selena Bright said. "Truth is, your recovery is due to your regenerative and self-healing enhancements more than anything we could do for you. You're alive because a kevlar plate in the bodysuit you wore deflected enough of the laser that hit you in the abdomen to limit the damage."

"I'm alive because of Ali," Coop corrected. "The missiles?"

"Paré and Tal took them down safely," Elie answered. "A team from the UEC collected everything left at Fordow. A thorough search of the entire complex is being conducted to make sure everything hidden is found."

"I certify you're alive," Dr. Bright said. "If I see you again Captain, I hope it isn't in another hospital bed."

The specialist left, leaving the mission team alone.

"Do you need to talk?" Elie asked.

"No," Coop replied.

"Good," Anton said, rising. "We have a shuttle to take us back to Tampa arriving soon. I expect you to walk onto it, Daniel Petraovich. Come, Hiro, we need to find a cafeteria."

The Russian departed, Hiro in his wake after giving Coop another, deeper, bow.

The Ethiopian moved next to Elie, looking down at Coop.

"I was hurt. I was angry. I was young. I'm over it," she told him. "What you did was the right thing to do. I get it now. I knew it then, but I was angry."

"I did not handle it well," Coop admitted. "I was a lot younger then, too."

Sindy leaned down to kiss Coop. "Get well. If you ever need my help, call."

She turned to Elie.

"You, too. You need me, you call," she told the Spaniard.

Elie hugged her fellow Ranger.

"Do you want to talk now?" she asked, waiting for the door to close behind Kebede.

"I've made mistakes, and people have died because of my mistakes," he said.

"You've been in battles, Coop," the Legionnaire said. A veteran of many bloody conflicts, an officer in charge of people who died under her watch, she understood his pain better than most. "Bad things happen when fighting starts. Things you cannot control. People die."

"I know, but I can be better," he said. "I can make better decisions, and be better prepared."

"Okay," she said, allowing him his personal space for grief and reflection. "I'll help."

The door opened and ENS Patterson entered.

"Hope this is an okay time," she said, observant to the mood in the recovery room.

"You're okay, Pam," Elie said. "Why are you in Kuwait?"

"Came in on the shuttle sent to take everyone home," she answered. "And get everyone's after-action reports. I have the four from the Team, and I have Paris Cassel's. I need Coop's. If he's up to it."

"I'm up to it," he answered. "Ready to record?"

"We have a situation."

"Fuck you, Connie," Booth said.

"Probably a poor choice of words," Director Patterson admitted. She handed her secure data pad to the Governor.

"Daniel Cooper's after-action report," she said, looking up at the spy master.

"I highlighted the important part," Patterson said.

Booth's eyes returned to the pad.

"Someone hired Berkel," she said. "Someone who knew he was a survivor of the Space Ranger Project, and he was a closet sociopath."

"Someone who knew about Fordow and the hidden MIRVs," Patterson added. "Someone with influence and access to secrets."

"Who did not get what they wanted, but might try again," Booth surmised. "You'll be watching?"

"Of course," the Director replied.

"Pam seems to have found her niche," Booth said, changing the subject.

"She's always refused to use me for leverage," Connie, speaking as a mother, said. "She even applied for the Naval Academy to set up her own path. Mother is a bureaucrat, so she opts for military service."

"And the Intelligence Service?"

"Proves she's still my daughter," Patterson answered, the pride obvious.

"If she remains with Myerson, and we continue to need the Space Rangers, which I have a feeling we will, she's in for an interesting future," Booth said.

END

GLOSSARY OF ABBREVIATIONS

EMS2   Earth-Moon Space Station.
Fixed orbital platform. Originally the launch point for missions to the moon and Mars. Enlarged to become the construction site for space vehicles.

ISS   International Space Station
Space lab in low orbit launched in 1998.

FAME   Fairchild Aerospace Martian Expeditions

M.I.T.   Massachusetts Institute of Technology

ETA   Estimated Time of Arrival
ETD   Estimated Time of Departure

EVA   Extravehicular Activity

DNI   Director of National Intelligence

CDC   Centers for Disease Control and Prevention

PDB   President's Daily Brief

GEIS   Global Emerging Infections Surveillance
www.geisglobalevents.org because it's real.

AFHSB   Armed Forces Health Surveillance Branch
https://health.mil/Military-Health-Topics/Health-Readiness/Armed-Forces-Health-Surveillance-Branch

DOD   Department of Defense

POTUS   President of the United States

PM   Prime Minister

PEOC   President's Emergency Operations Center
https://whitehouse.gov1.info/tunnel/

IDF   Israeli Defense Forces

AWS   Autonomous Weapons System
LAWS   Lethal Autonomous Weapons System

C.diff   Clostridium difficile Infection
http://www.mayoclinic.org/diseases-conditions/c-difficile/
home/ovc-20202264

MARV   Marburg Virus
http://www.who.int/mediacentre/factsheets/fs_marburg/
en/

NFO   Naval Flight Officer

PFC   Private First Class
SPC   Specialist
NCO   Non-Commissioned Officer
WO   Warrant Officer

SO	Special Operations
KIA	Killed In Action
MIA	Missing In Action
BDU	Battlefield Dress Uniform
RAT	Recon All-Terrain Transport
AT/ATV	All-Terrain Vehicle
S&R	Search and Rescue (Assumed Alive)
	Search and Recovery (Assumed Dead)
RPG	Rocket Propelled Grenades
SIT-REP	Situation Report
GPS	Global Positioning System
SOS	Internationally Recognized Distress Signal
UEC	United Earth Council
DNA	Deoxyribonucleic Acid
RNA	Ribonucleic Acid
PSY-OPS	Psychological Operations

SCUBA	Self-Contained Underwater Breathing Apparatus
HALO	High Altitude - Low Opening
LALA	Low Altitude - Low Opening
CQB	Close Quarters Battle
SERE	Survival - Escape - Resistance - Evasion
SEAL	"Sea, Air, and Land" Teams / Navy Special Ops
UESE	United Earth Security Establishment
MIRV	Multiple Independently Targetable Reentry Vehicle

http://nsarchive.gwu.edu/nsa/NC/mirv/mirv.html

SP	Shore Patrol
MP	Military Police
CIC	Command and Intelligence Centers
COMS	Communications
OPS	Operations and Planning
EMP	Electromagnetic Pulse

SPACE RANGERS

Titus Andronicus Barnwell, Junior. "Tab"
United States
Can-Am Marines / Intelligence

Rolf Garen Berkel
Germany
Bundeswehr - Rapid Forces Division
    KSK (Kommando Spezialkräfte)

Alessandra Isadora Campos. "Ali"
Brazil
Brazilian National Security Service

Elena Fallon Casalobos. "Elie"
    Pilot Callsign: Loba
Spanish
Spanish 19th Special Operations Group /
    Caballero Legionario Maderal Oleaga

Thomas Benedict Claflin. "Benny"
United Kingdom
British Army / Special Air Service

Daniel Marcel Cooper. "Coop"
Father: US Mother: Canadian
Can-Am Army Rangers.

Anton Nikolai Gregory.
Russian
Special Operations Forces of the Federation Armed Forces

Samuel Elsworth Harrington. "Sam"
United Kingdom
Royal Air Force

Senait Kebede. "Sindy"
Ethiopian
National Defense Force / Special Forces Commando

Hiroshi Kimura. "Hiro"
Japanese
Japanese National Police / Imperial Guard

Antoniette Rachelle Paré.
    Pilot Callsign: Rain
French Canadian
Can-Am Navy

Noa Mariamne Tal.
    Pilot Callsign: Sabre
Israel
Israeli Defense Forces / Unit 5700

More interesting information at donfoxe.com

www.ingramcontent.com/pod-product-compliance
Lightning Source LLC
Chambersburg PA
CBHW022010170626
46808CB00001B/347